A PROBLEM IN COMMUNICATION

"I won't talk without a lawyer," Don answered firmly.

"No? I'm sorry. Don, in setting up your interview I budgeted eleven minutes for nonsense. You have used up four already—no; five. When the eleven minutes are gone and you find yourself spitting out teeth, remember that I bore you no malice. Now about this matter of whether or not you will talk; there are several ways of making a man talk and each method has its fans. Drugs, for example—nitrous oxide, scopolamine, sodium pentothal, not to mention some of the new, more subtle and relatively non-toxic developments. Even alcohols have been used with great success by intelligence operatives.

"And there is hypnosis and its many variations. There is also the artificial stimulation of an unbearable need. Finally there is old-fashioned force —pain." The security officer glanced at his watch and added, "Only thirty seconds of nonsense still available, Don. Shall we start?"

"Huh? You used up the time; I've hardly said a word."

"I haven't time to be fair. . . ."

Also by Robert A. Heinlein
published by Ballantine Books:

ROCKET SHIP GALILEO

SPACE CADET

RED PLANET

FARMER IN THE SKY

THE ROLLING STONES

STARMAN JONES

THE STAR BEAST

TUNNEL IN THE SKY

TIME FOR THE STARS

CITIZEN OF THE GALAXY

HAVE SPACE SUIT—WILL TRAVEL

Between Planets

Robert A. Heinlein

A Del Rey Book

BALLANTINE BOOKS • NEW YORK

For SCOTT and KENT

A Del Rey Book
Published by Ballantine Books

A condensed version under the title *Planets in Combat* appeared
in three parts in *Blue Book Magazine*.

ISBN 0-345-27796-1

This edition published by arrangement with Charles Scribner's
Sons

Manufactured in the United States of America

First Ballantine Books Edition: February 1978
Third Printing: May 1978

Cover illustration by Darrell Sweet

CONTENTS

I

New Mexico

"Easy, boy, easy!"

Don Harvey reined in the fat little cow pony. Ordinarily Lazy lived up to his name; today he seemed to want to go places. Don hardly blamed him. It was such a day as comes only to New Mexico, with sky scrubbed clean by a passing shower, the ground already dry but with a piece of rainbow still hanging in the distance. The sky was too blue, the buttes too rosy, and the far reaches too sharp to be quite convincing. Incredible peace hung over the land and with it a breathless expectancy of something wonderful about to happen.

"We've got all day," he cautioned Lazy, "so don't get yourself in a lather. That's a stiff climb ahead." Don was riding alone because he had decked out Lazy in a magnificent Mexican saddle his parents had ordered sent to him for his birthday. It was a beautiful thing, as gaudy with silver as an Indian buck, but it was as out of place at the ranch school he attended as formal clothes at a branding—a point which his parents had not realized. Don was proud of it, but the other boys rode plain stock saddles; they kidded him unmercifully and had turned "Donald James Harvey" into "Don Jaime" when he first appeared with it.

Lazy suddenly shied. Don glanced around, spotted the cause, whipped out his gun, and fired. He then dismounted, throwing the reins forward so that Lazy would stand, and examined his work. In the shadow of a rock a fair-sized snake, seven rattles on its tail, was still twitching. Its head lay by it, burned off. Don decided not to save the rattles; had he pinpointed the head he would have taken it in to show his marksmanship. As it was, he had been forced to slice sidewise with the beam before he got it. If he brought in a snake killed in such a clumsy fashion someone would be sure to ask him why he hadn't used a garden hose.

He let it lie and remounted while talking to Lazy. "Just a no-good old sidewinder," he said reassuringly. "More scared of you than you were of it."

He clucked and they started off. A few hundred yards further on Lazy shied again, not from a snake this time but from an unexpected noise. Don pulled him in and spoke severely. "You bird-brained butterball! When are you going to learn not to jump when the telephone rings?"

Lazy twitched his shoulder muscles and snorted. Don reached for the pommel, removed the phone, and answered. "Mobile 6-J-233309, Don Harvey speaking."

"Mr. Reeves, Don," came back the voice of the headmaster of Ranchito Alegre. "Where are you?"

"Headed up Peddler's Grave Mesa, sir."

"Get home as quickly as you can."

"Uh, what's up, sir?"

"Radiogram from your parents. I'll send the copter out for you if the cook is back—with someone to bring your horse in."

Don hesitated. He didn't want just anybody to ride Lazy, like as not getting him overheated and failing to cool him off. On the other hand a radio from his folks could not help but be important. His parents were on Mars and his mother wrote regularly, every ship—but radiograms, other than Christmas and birthday greetings, were almost unheard of.

"I'll hurry, sir."

"Right!" Mr. Reeves switched off. Don turned Lazy and headed back down the trail. Lazy seemed disappointed and looked back accusingly.

As it turned out, they were only a half mile from the school when the ranch copter spotted them. Don waved it off and took Lazy on in himself. Despite his curiosity he delayed to wipe down the pony and water it before he went in. Mr. Reeves was waiting in his office and motioned for him to come in. He handed Don the message.

It read: DEAR SON, PASSAGE RESERVED FOR YOU VALKYRIE CIRCUM-TERRA TWELVE APRIL LOVE—MOTHER AND DAD.

Don blinked at it, having trouble taking in the simple facts. "But that's right away!"

"Yes. You weren't expecting it?"

Don thought it over. He had halfway expected to go home—if one could call it going home when he had never set foot on Mars—at the end of the school year. If they had arranged his passage for the *Vanderdecken* three months from now . . . "Uh, not exactly. I can't figure out why they would send for me before the end of the term."

Mr. Reeves fitted his finger tips carefully together. "I'd say that it was obvious."

Don looked startled. "You mean? Mr. Reeves, you don't really think there is going to be trouble, do you?"

The headmaster answered gravely, "Don, I'm not a prophet. But it is my guess that your parents are sufficiently worried that they want you out of a potential war zone as quickly as possible."

He was still having trouble readjusting. Wars were something you studied, not something that actually happened. Of course his class in contemporary history had kept track of the current crisis in colonial affairs, but, even so, it had seemed something far away, even for one as widely traveled as himself—a matter for diplomats and politicians, not something real.

"Look, Mr. Reeves, they may be jumpy but I'm not. I'd like to send a radio telling them that I'll be along on the next ship, as soon as school is out."

Mr. Reeves shook his head. "No. I can't let you go against your parents' explicit instructions. In the second place, ah—" The headmaster seemed to have difficulty in choosing his words. "—that is to say, Donald, in the event of war, you might find your position here, shall we call it, uncomfortable?"

A bleak wind seemed to have found its way into the

office. Don felt lonely and older than he should feel. "Why?" he asked gruffly.

Mr. Reeves studied his fingernails. "Are you quite sure where your loyalties lie?" he said slowly.

Don forced himself to think about it. His father had been born on Earth; his mother was a second-generation Venus colonial. But neither planet was truly their home; they had met and married on Luna and had pursued their researches in planetology in many sectors of the solar system. Don himself had been born out in space and his birth certificate, issued by the Federation, had left the question of his nationality open. He could claim dual citizenship by parental derivation. He did not think of himself as a Venus colonial; it had been so long since his family had last visited Venus that the place had grown unreal in his mind. On the other hand he had been eleven years old before he had ever rested his eyes on the lovely hills of Earth.

"I'm a citizen of the System," he said harshly.

"Mmmm—" said the headmaster. "That's a fine phrase and perhaps someday it will mean something. In the meantime, speaking as a friend, I agree with your parents. Mars is likely to be neutral territory; you'll be safe there. Again, speaking as your friend—things may get a little rough here for anyone whose loyalty is not perfectly clear."

"Nobody has any business questioning my loyalty! Under the law, I count as native born!"

The man did not answer. Don burst out, "The whole thing is silly! If the Federation wasn't trying to bleed Venus white there wouldn't be any war talk."

Reeves stood up. "That will be all, Don. I'm not going to argue politics with you."

"It's true! Read Chamberlain's *Theory of Colonial Expansion!*"

Reeves seemed startled. "Where did you lay hands on *that* book? Not in the school library."

Don did not answer. His father had sent it to him but had cautioned him not to let it be seen; it was one of the suppressed books—on Earth, at least. Reeves went on, "Don, have you been dealing with a *booklegger?*"

Don remained silent. "Answer me!"

Presently Reeves took a deep breath and said, "Never mind. Go up to your room and pack. The copter will take you to Albuquerque at one o'clock."

"Yes, sir." He had started to leave when the headmaster called him back.

"Just a moment. In the heat of our, uh, discussion I almost forgot that there was a second message for you."

"Oh?" Don accepted the slip; it said: DEAR SON, BE SURE TO SAY GOODBYE TO UNCLE DUDLEY BEFORE YOU LEAVE—MOTHER.

This second message surprised him in some ways even more than the first; he had trouble realizing that his mother must mean Dr. Dudley Jefferson—a friend of his parents but no relation, and a person of no importance in his own life. But Reeves seemed not to see anything odd in the message, so he stuck it in his Levis and left the room.

Long as he had been earthbound he approached packing with a true spaceman's spirit. He knew that his passage would entitle him to only fifty pounds of free lift; he started discarding right and left. Shortly he had two piles, a very small one on his own bed—indispensable clothing, a few capsules of microfilm, his slide rule, a stylus, and a *vreetha*, a flutelike Martian instrument which he had not played in a long time as his schoolmates had objected. On his roommate's bed was a much larger pile of discards.

He picked up the *vreetha*, tried a couple of runs, and put it on the larger pile. Taking a Martian product to Mars was coal to Newcastle. His roommate, Jack Moreau, came in as he did so. "What in time goes on? Housecleaning?"

"Leaving."

Jack dug a finger into his ear. "I must be getting deaf. I could have sworn you said you were leaving."

"I am." Don stopped and explained, showing Jack the message from his parents.

Jack looked distressed. "I don't like this. Of course I knew this was our last year, but I didn't figure on you jumping the gun. I probably won't sleep without your snores to soothe me. What's the rush?"

"I don't know. I really don't. The Head says that my folks

have war jitters and want to drag their little darling to safety. But that's silly, don't you think? I mean, people are too civilized to go to war today."

Jack did not answer. Don waited, then said sharply, "You agree, don't you? There won't be any war."

Jack answered slowly, "Could be. Or maybe not."

"Oh, come off it!"

His roommate answered, "Want me to help you pack?"

"There isn't anything to pack."

"How about all that stuff?"

"That's yours, if you want it. Pick it over, then call in the others and let them take what they like."

"Huh? Gee, Don, I don't want your stuff. I'll pack it and ship it after you."

"Ever ship anything 'tween planets? It's not worth it."

"Then sell it. Tell you what, we'll hold an auction right after supper."

Don shook his head. "No time. I'm leaving at one o'clock."

"What? You're really blitzing me, kid. I don't like this."

"Can't be helped." He turned back to his sorting.

Several of his friends drifted in to say goodbye. Don himself had not spread the news and he did not suppose that the headmaster would have talked, yet somehow the grapevine had spread the word. He invited them to help themselves to the plunder, subject to Jack's prior claim.

Presently he noticed that none of them asked why he was leaving. It bothered him more than if they had talked about it. He wanted to tell someone, anyone, that it was ridiculous to doubt his loyalty—and anyhow there wasn't going to be a war!

Rupe Salter, a boy from another wing, stuck his head in, looked over the preparations. "Running out, eh? I heard you were and thought I'd check up."

"I'm leaving, if that's what you mean."

"That's what I said. See here, 'Don Jaime,' how about that circus saddle of yours? I'll take it off your hands if the price is right."

"It's not for sale."

"Huh? No horses where you're going. Make me a price."

"It belongs to Jack here."

"And it's still not for sale," Moreau answered promptly.

"Like that, eh? Suit yourself." Salter went on blandly, "Another thing—you willed that nag of yours yet?"

The boys' mounts, with few exceptions, were owned by the school, but it was a cherished and long-standing privilege of a boy graduating to "will" his temporary ownership to a boy of his choice. Don looked up sharply; until that moment he had not thought about Lazy. He realized with sudden grief that he could not take the little fat clown with him—nor had he made any arrangements for his welfare. "The matter is settled," he answered, added to himself: as far as *you* are concerned.

"Who gets him? I could make it worth your while. He's not much of a horse, but I want to get rid of the goat I've had to put up with."

"It's settled."

"Be sensible. I can see the Head and get him anyhow. Willing a horse is a graduating privilege and you're ducking out ahead of time."

"Get out!"

Salter grinned. "Touchy, aren't you? Just like all fogeaters, too touchy to know what's good for you. Well, you're going to be taught a lesson some day soon."

Don, already on edge, was too angry to trust himself to speak. "Fog-eater," used to describe a man from cloudwrapped Venus, was merely ragging, no worse than "Limey" or "Yank"—unless the tone of voice and context made it, as now, a deliberate insult. The others looked at him, half expecting action.

Jack got up hastily from the bed and went toward Salter. "Get going, Salty. We're too busy to monkey around with you." Salter looked at Don, then back at Jack, shrugged and said, "I'm too busy to hang around here . . . but not *too* busy, if you have anything in mind."

The noon bell pealed from the mess hall; it broke the tension. Several boys started for the door; Salter moved out with them. Don hung back. Jack said, "Come on—beans!"

"Jack?"

"Yeah?"

"How about you taking over Lazy?"

"Gee, Don! I'd like to accommodate you—but what would I do with Lady Maude?"

"Uh, I guess so. What'll I do?"

"Let me see—" Jack's face brightened. "You know that kid Squinty Morris? The new kid from Manitoba? He hasn't got a permanent yet; he's been taking his rotation with the goats. He'd treat Lazy right; I know, I let him try Maudie once. He's got gentle hands."

Don looked relieved. "Will you fix it for me? And see Mr. Reeves?"

"Huh? You can see him at lunch; come on."

"I'm not going to lunch. I'm not hungry. And I don't much want to talk to the Head about it."

"Why not?"

"Well, I don't know. When he called me in this morning he didn't seem exactly . . . friendly."

"What did he say?"

"It wasn't his words; it was his manner. Maybe I *am* touchy—but I sort of thought he was glad to see me go."

Don expected Jack to object, convince him that he was wrong. Instead he was silent for a moment, then said quietly, "Don't take it too hard, Don. The Head is probably edgy too. You know he's got his orders?"

"Huh? What orders?"

"You knew he was a reserve officer, didn't you? He put in for orders and got 'em, effective at end of term. Mrs. Reeves is taking over the school—for the duration."

Don, already overstrained, felt his head whirling. For the duration? How could anyone say that when there wasn't any such thing? " 'Sfact," Jack went on. "I got it straight from cookie." He paused, then went on, "See here, old son—we're pals, aren't we?"

"Huh? Sure, sure!"

"Then give it to me straight: are you actually going to Mars? Or are you heading for Venus to sign up?"

"Whatever gave you that notion?"

"Skip it, then. Believe me; it wouldn't make any difference between us. My old man says that when it's time to be counted, the important thing is to be man enough to stand up." He looked at Don's face, then went on, "What you do about it is up to you. You know I've got a birthday coming up next month?"

"Huh? Yes, so you have."

"Come then, I'm going to sign up for pilot training. That's why I wanted to know what you planned to do."

"Oh—"

"But it doesn't make any difference—not between us. Anyhow, you're going to Mars."

"Yes. Yes, that's right."

"Good!" Jack glanced at his watch. "I've got to run—or they'll throw my chow to the pigs. Sure you're not coming?"

"Sure."

"See you." He dashed out.

Don stood for a moment, rearranging his ideas. Old Jack must be taking this seriously—giving up Yale for pilot training. But he was wrong—he *had* to be wrong.

Presently he went out to the corral.

Lazy answered his call, then started searching his pockets for sugar. "Sorry, old fellow," he said sadly, "not even a carrot. I forgot." He stood with his face to the horse's cheek and scratched the beast's ears. He talked to it in low tones, explaining as carefully as if Lazy could understand all the difficult words.

"So that's how it is," he concluded. "I've got to go away and they won't let me take you with me." He thought back to the day their association had begun. Lazy had been hardly more than a colt, but Don had been frightened of him. He seemed huge, dangerous, probably carnivorous. He had never seen a horse before coming to Earth; Lazy was the first he had ever seen close up.

Suddenly he choked, could talk no further. He flung his arms around the horse's neck and leaked tears.

Lazy nickered softly, knowing that something was wrong, and tried to nuzzle him. Don raised his head. "Goodbye, boy. Take care of yourself." He turned abruptly and ran toward the dormitories.

II

"Mene, Mene, Tekel, Upharsin"

DANIEL V:25

THE SCHOOL copter dumped him down at the Albuquerque field. He had to hurry to catch his rocket as traffic control had required them to swing wide around Sandia Weapons Center. When he weighed in he ran into another new security wrinkle. "Got a camera in that stuff, son?" the weighmaster had inquired as he passed over his bags.

"No. Why?"

"Because we'll fog your film when we fluoroscope, that's why." Apparently X-ray failed to show any bombs hidden in his underwear; his bags were handed back and he went aboard—the winged-rocket *Santa Fé Trail*, shuttling between the Southwest and New Chicago. Inside, he fastened his safety belts, snuggled down into the cushions, and waited.

At first the noise of the blast-off bothered him more than the pressure. But the noise dopplered away as they passed the speed of sound while the acceleration grew worse; he blacked out.

He came to as the ship went into free flight, arching in a high parabola over the plains. At once he felt great relief no longer to have unbearable weight racking his rib cage, straining his heart, turning his muscles to water—but, before he could enjoy the blessed relief, he was aware of a new sensation; his stomach was trying to crawl up his gullet.

At first he was alarmed, being unable to account for the unexpected and unbearably unpleasant sensation. Then he had a sudden wild suspicion—could it? Oh, no! It *couldn't* be . . . not space sickness, not to *him*. Why, he had been born in free fall; space nausea was for Earth crawlers, groundhogs!

But the suspicion grew to certainty; years of easy living on a planet had worn out his immunity. With secret embarrassment he conceded that he certainly was acting like a groundhog. It had not occurred to him to ask for an anti-nausea shot before blast-off, though he had walked past the counter plainly marked with a red cross.

Shortly his secret embarrassment became public; he had barely time to get at the plastic container provided for the purpose. Thereafter he felt better, although weak, and listened half-heartedly to the canned description coming out of the loudspeaker of the country over which they were falling. Presently, near Kansas City, the sky turned from black back to purple again, the air foils took hold, and the passengers again felt weight as the rocket continued glider fashion on a long, screaming approach to New Chicago. Don folded his couch into a chair and sat up.

Twenty minutes later, as the field came up to meet them, rocket units in the nose were triggered by radar and the *Santa Fé Trail* braked to a landing. The entire trip had taken less time than the copter jaunt from the school to Alburquerque—something less than an hour for the same route eastward that the covered wagons had made westward in eighty days, with luck. The local rocket landed on a field just outside the city, next door to the enormous field, still slightly radioactive, which was both the main spaceport of the planet and the former site of Old Chicago.

Don hung back and let a Navajo family disembark ahead of him, then followed the squaw out. A movable slideway had crawled out to the ship; he stepped on it and let it carry him into the station. Once inside he was confused by the bustling size of the place, level after level, above and below ground. Gary Station served not merely the *Santa Fé Trail*, the *Route 66*, and other local rockets shuttling to the Southwest; it served a dozen other local lines, as well as ocean hoppers, freight tubes, and space ships operating between Earth and Circum-Terra Station—and thence to Luna, Venus, Mars, and the Jovian moons; it was the spinal cord of a more-than-world-wide empire.

Tuned as he was to the wide and empty New Mexico desert and, before that, to the wider wastes of space Don felt oppressed and irritated by the noisy swarming mass. He felt the loss of dignity that comes from men behaving like ants, even though his feeling was not thought out in words. Still, it had to be faced—he spotted the triple globes of Interplanet Lines and followed glowing arrows to its reservation office.

An uninterested clerk assured him that the office had no record of his reservation in the *Valkyrie*. Patiently Don explained that the reservation had been made from Mars and displayed the radiogram from his parents. Annoyed into activity the clerk finally consented to phone Circum-Terra; the satellite station confirmed the reservation. The clerk signed off and turned back to Don. "Okay, you can pay for it here."

Don had a sinking feeling. "I thought it was already paid for?" He had on him his father's letter-of-credit but it was not enough to cover passage to Mars.

"Huh? They didn't say anything about it being prepaid."

At Don's insistence the clerk again phoned the space station. Yes, the passage was prepaid since it had been placed from the other end; didn't the clerk know his tariff book? Thwarted on all sides, the clerk grudgingly issued Don a ticket to couch 64, Rocket Ship *Glory Road*, lifting from Earth for Circum-Terra at 9:03:57 the following morning. "Got your security clearance?"

"Huh? What's that?"

The clerk appeared to gloat at what was a legitimate opportunity to decline to do business after all. He withdrew the ticket. "Don't you bother to follow the news? Give me your ID."

Reluctantly Don passed over his identity card; the clerk stuck it in a stat machine and handed it back. "Now your thumb prints."

Don impressed them and said, "Is that all? Can I have my ticket?"

" 'Is that all?' he says! Be here about an hour early tomorrow morning. You can pick up your ticket then—provided the I.B.I. says you can."

The clerk turned away. Don, feeling forlorn, did likewise. He did not know quite what to do next. He had told Headmaster Reeves that he would stay overnight at the *Hilton Caravansary*, that being the hotel his family had stopped at years earlier and the only one he knew by name. On the other hand he had to attempt to locate Dr. Jefferson—"Uncle Dudley"—since his mother had made such a point of it. It was still early afternoon; he decided to check his bags and start looking.

Bags disposed of, he found an empty communication booth and looked up the doctor's code, punched it into the machine. The doctor's phone regretted politely that Dr. Jefferson was not at home and requested him to leave a message. He was dictating it when a warm voice interrupted: "I'm at home to you, Donald. Where are you, lad?" The view screen cut in and he found himself looking at the somewhat familiar features of Dr. Dudley Jefferson.

"Oh! I'm at the station, Doctor—Gary Station. I just got in."

"Then grab a cab and come here at once."

"Uh, I don't want to put you to any trouble, Doctor. I called because mother said to say goodbye to you." Privately he had hoped that Dr. Jefferson would be too busy to waste time on him. Much as he disapproved of cities he did not want to spend his last night on Earth exchanging politeness with a family friend; he wanted to stir around and find out just what the modern Babylon did have to offer in the way of diversion. His letter-of-credit was burning a hole in his pocket; he wanted to bleed it a bit.

"No trouble! See you in a few minutes. Meanwhile I'll pick out a fatted calf and butcher it. By the way, did you receive a package from me?" The doctor looked suddenly intent.

"A package? No."

Dr. Jefferson muttered something about the mail service. Don said, "Maybe it will catch up with me. Was it important?"

"Uh, never mind; we'll speak of it later. You left a forwarding address?"

"Yes, sir—the *Caravansary*."

"Well—whip up the horses and see how quickly you can get here. Open sky!"

"And safe grounding, sir." They both switched off. Don left the booth and looked around for a cab stand. The station seemed more jammed than ever, with uniforms much

in evidence, not only those of pilots and other ship person-
nel but military uniforms of many corps—and always the
ubiquitous security police. Don fought his way through the
crowd, down a ramp, along a slidewalk tunnel, and finally
found what he wanted. There was a queue waiting for
cabs; he joined it.

Beside the queue was sprawled the big, ungainly saurian
form of a Venerian "dragon." When Don progressed in line
until he was beside it, he politely whistled a greeting.

The dragon swiveled one fluttering eyestalk in his direction. Strapped to the "chest" of the creature, between its
forelegs and immediately below and in reach of its handling
tendrils, was a small box, a voder. The tendrils writhed
over the keys and the Venerian answered him, via mechanical voder speech, rather than by whistling in his own
language. "Greetings to you also, young sir. It is pleasant
indeed, among strangers, to hear the sounds one heard in
the egg." Don noted with delight that the outlander had a
distinctly Cockney accent in the use of his machine.

He whistled his thanks and a hope that the dragon
might die pleasantly.

The Venerian thanked him, again with the voder, and
added, "Charming as is your accent, will you do me the
favor of using your own speech that I may practice it?"

Don suspected that his modulation was so atrocious that
the Venerian could hardly understand it; he lapsed at once
into human words. "My name is Don Harvey," he replied
and whistled once more—but just to give his own Venerian
name, "Mist on the Waters"; it had been selected by his
mother and he saw nothing funny about it.

Nor did the dragon. He whistled for the first time, nam-
ing himself, and added via voder, "I am called 'Sir Isaac
Newton.' " Don understood that the Venerian, in so tagging
himself, was following the common dragon custom of bor-
rowing as a name of convenience the name of some earth-
human admired by the borrower.

Don wanted to ask "Sir Isaac Newton" if by chance he
knew Don's mother's family, but the queue was moving up
and the dragon was lying still; he was forced to move
along to keep from losing his place in line. The Venerian

followed him with one oscillating eye and whistled that he hoped that Don, too, might die pleasantly.

There was an interruption in the flow of autocabs to the stand; a man-operated flatbed truck drew up and let down a ramp. The dragon reared up on six sturdy legs and climbed aboard. Don whistled a farewell—and became suddenly and unpleasantly aware that a security policeman was giving him undivided attention. He was glad to crawl into his autocab and close the cover.

He dialed the address and settled back. The little car lurched forward, climbed a ramp, threaded through a freight tunnel, and mounted an elevator. At first Don tried to keep track of where it was taking him but the tortured convolutions of the ant hill called "New Chicago" would have made a topologist dyspeptic; he gave up. The robot cab seemed to know where it was going and, no doubt, the master machine from which it received its signals knew. Don spent the rest of the trip fretting over the fact that his ticket had not yet been turned over to him, over the unwelcome attention of the security policeman, and, finally, about the package from Dr. Jefferson. The last did not worry him; it simply annoyed him to have mail go astray. He hoped that Mr. Reeves would realize that any mail not forwarded by this afternoon would have to follow him all the way to Mars.

Then he thought about "Sir Isaac." It was nice to run across somebody from home.

Dr. Jefferson's apartment turned out to be far underground in an expensive quarter of the city. Don almost failed to arrive; the cab had paused at the apartment door but when he tried to get out the door would not open. This reminded him that he must first pay the fare shown in the meter—only to discover that he had pulled the bumpkin trick of engaging a robot vehicle without having coins on him to feed the meter. He was sure that the little car, clever as it was, would not even deign to sniff at his letter-of-credit. He was expecting disconsolately to be carted by the machine off to the nearest police station when he was rescued by the appearance of Dr. Jefferson.

The doctor gave him coins to pay the shot and ushered him in. "Think nothing of it, my boy; it happens to me about once a week. The local desk sergeant keeps a drawer full of hard money just to buy me out of hock from our mechanical masters. I pay him off once a quarter, cumshaw additional. Sit down. Sherry?"

"Er, no, thank you, sir."

"Coffee, then. Cream and sugar at your elbow. What do you hear from your parents?"

"Why, the usual things. Both well and working hard and all that." Don looked around him as he spoke. The room was large, comfortable, even luxurious, although books spilling lavishly and untidily over shelves and tables and even chairs masked its true richness. What appeared to be a real fire burned in one corner. Through an open door he could see several more rooms. He made a high, and grossly inadequate, mental estimate of the cost of such an establishment in New Chicago.

Facing them was a view window which should have looked into the bowels of the city; instead it reflected a mountain stream and fir trees. A trout broke water as he watched.

"I'm sure they are working hard," his host answered. "They always do. Your father is attempting to seek out, in one short lifetime, secrets that have been piling up for millions of years. Impossible—but he makes a good stab at it. Son, do you realize that when your father started his career we hadn't even dreamed that the first system empire ever existed?" He added thoughtfully, "If it was the first." He went on, "Now we have felt out the ruins on the floor of two oceans—and tied them in with records from four other planets. Of course your father didn't do it all, or even most of it—but his work has been indispensable. Your father is a great man, Donald—and so is your mother. When I speak of either one I really mean the team. Help yourself to sandwiches."

Don said, "Thank you," and did so, thereby avoiding a direct answer. He was warmly pleased to hear his parents praised but it did not seem to be quite the thing to agree heartily.

But the doctor was capable of carrying on the conversation unassisted. "Of course we may never know all the answers. How was the noblest planet of them all, the home of empire, broken and dispersed into space junk? Your father spent four years in the Asteroid Belt—you were along, weren't you?—and never found a firm answer to that. Was it a paired planet, like Earth-Luna, and broken up by tidal strains? Or was it blown up?"

"Blown up?" Don protested. "But that's theoretically impossible—isn't it?"

Dr. Jefferson brushed it aside. "Everything is theoretically impossible, until it's done. One could write a history of science in reverse by assembling the solemn pronouncements of highest authority about what could not be done and could never happen. Studied any mathematical philosophy, Don? Familiar with infinite universe sheafs and open-ended postulate systems?"

"Uh, I'm afraid not, sir."

"Simple idea and very tempting. The notion that everything is possible—and I mean everything—and everything has happened. *Everything.* One universe in which you accepted that wine and got drunk as a skunk. Another in which the fifth planet never broke up. Another in which atomic power and nuclear weapons are as impossible as our ancestors thought they were. That last one might have its points, for sissies at least. Like me."

He stood up. "Don't eat too many sandwiches. I'm going to take you out to a restaurant where there will be food, among other things . . . and such food as Zeus promised the gods—and failed to deliver."

"I don't want to take up too much of your time, sir." Don was still hoping to get out on the town by himself. He had a dismaying vision of dinner in some stuffy rich man's club, followed by an evening of highfalutin talk. And it *was* his last night on Earth.

"Time? What is time? Each hour ahead is as fresh as was the one we just used. You registered at the *Caravansary?*"

"No, sir, I just checked my bags at the station."

"Good. You'll stay here tonight; we'll send for your luggage later." Dr. Jefferson's manner changed slightly. "But your mail was to be sent to the hotel?"

"That's right."

Don was surprised to see that Dr. Jefferson looked distinctly worried. "Well, we'll check into that later. That package I sent to you—would it be forwarded promptly?"

"I really don't know, sir. Ordinarily the mail comes in twice a day. If it came in after I left, it would ordinarily wait over until morning. But if the headmaster thought about it, he might have it sent into town special so that I would get it before up-ship tomorrow morning."

"Mean to say there isn't a tube into the school?"

"No, sir, the cook brings in the morning mail when he shops and the afternoon mail is chuted in by the Roswell copter bus."

"A desert island! Well . . . we'll check around midnight. If it hasn't arrived then—never mind." Nevertheless he seemed perturbed and hardly spoke during their ride to dinner.

The restaurant was misnamed *The Back Room* and there was no sign out to indicate its location; it was simply one of many doors in a side tunnel. Nevertheless many people seemed to know where it was and to be anxious to get in, only to be thwarted by a stern-faced dignitary guarding a velvet rope. This ambassador recognized Dr. Jefferson and sent for the *maître d'hôtel*. The doctor made a gesture understood by headwaiters throughout history, the rope was dropped, and they were conducted in royal progress to a ringside table. Don was bug-eyed at the size of the bribe. Thus he was ready with the proper facial expression when he caught sight of their waitress.

His reaction to her was simple; she was, it seemed to him, the most beautiful sight he had ever seen, both in person and in costume. Dr. Jefferson caught his expression and chuckled. "Don't use up your enthusiasm, son. The ones we have paid to see will be out there." He waved at the floor. "Cocktail first?"

Don said that he didn't believe so, thank you.

"Suit yourself. You are man high and a single taste of the fleshpots wouldn't do you any permanent harm. But suppose you let me order dinner for us?" Don agreed. While

Dr. Jefferson was consulting with the captive princess over the menu, Don looked around. The room simulated out-doors in the late evening; stars were just appearing over-head. A high brick wall ran around the room, hiding the non-existent middle distance and patching in the floor to the false sky. Apple trees hung over the wall and stirred in the breeze. An old-fashioned well with a well sweep stood beyond the tables on the far side of the room; Don saw another "captive princess" go to it, operate the sweep, and remove a silver pail containing a wrapped bottle.

At the ringside opposite them a table had been removed to make room for a large transparent plastic capsule on wheels. Don had never seen one but he recognized its func-tion; it was a Martian's "perambulator," a portable air-con-ditioning unit to provide the rare, cold air necessary to a Martian aborigine. The occupant could be seen dimly, his frail body supported by a metal articulated servo frame-work to assist him in coping with the robust gravity of the third planet. His pseudo wings drooped sadly and he did not move. Don felt sorry for him.

As a youngster he had met Martians on Luna, but Luna's feeble field was less than that of Mars; it did not turn them into cripples, paralyzed by a gravity field too painful for their evolutionary pattern. It was both difficult and dangerous for a Martian to risk coming to Earth; Don won-dered what had induced this one. A diplomatic mission, perhaps?

Dr. Jefferson dismissed the waitress, looked up and noticed him staring at the Martian. Don said, "I was just wonder-ing why he would come here. Not to eat, surely."

"Probably wants to watch the animals feeding. That's part of my own reason, Don. Take a good look around you; you'll never see the like again."

"No, I guess not—not on Mars."

"That's not what I mean. Sodom and Gomorrah, lad—rot-ten at the core and skidding toward the pit. '—these our ac-tors, as I foretold you . . . are melted into air—' and so forth. Perhaps even 'the great globe itself.' I talk too much. En-joy it; it won't last long."

Don looked puzzled. "Dr. Jefferson, do you *like* living here?"

"Me? I'm as decadent as the city I infest; it's my natural element. But that doesn't keep me from telling a hawk from a handsaw."

The orchestra, which had been playing softly from nowhere in particular, stopped suddenly and the sound system announced "News flash!" At the same time the darkening sky overhead turned black and lighted letters started marching across it. The voice over the sound system read aloud the words streaming across the ceiling: BERMUDA: OFFICIAL: THE DEPARTMENT OF COLONIAL AFFAIRS HAS JUST ANNOUNCED THAT THE PROVISIONAL COMMITTEE OF THE VENUS COLONIES HAS REJECTED OUR NOTE. A SOURCE CLOSE TO THE FEDERATION CHAIRMAN SAYS THAT THIS IS AN EXPECTED DEVELOPMENT AND NO CAUSE FOR ALARM.

The lights went up and the music resumed. Dr. Jefferson's lips were stretched back in a mirthless grin. "How appropriate!" he commented. "How timely! The handwriting on the wall."

Don started to blurt out a comment, but was distracted by the start of the show. The stage floor by them had sunk out of sight, unnoticed, during the news flash. Now from the pit thus created came a drifting, floating cloud lighted from within with purple and flame and rose. The cloud melted away and Don could see that the stage was back in place and peopled with dancers. There was a mountain in the stage background.

Dr. Jefferson had been right; the ones worth staring at were on the stage, not serving the tables. Don's attention was so taken that he did not notice that food had been placed in front of him. His host touched his elbow. "Eat something, before you faint."

"Huh? Oh, yes, sir!" He did so, busily and with good appetite but with his eyes on the entertainers. There was one man in the cast, portraying Tannhäuser, but Don did not know and did not care whom he represented; he noticed him only when he got in the way. Similarly, he had finished two thirds of what was placed before him without noticing what he was eating.

Dr. Jefferson said, "Like it?"

Don did a double-take and realized that the doctor was speaking of food, not of the dancers. "Oh, yes! It's awfully good." He examined his plate. "But what is it?"

"Don't you recognize it? Baked baby gregarian."

It took a couple of seconds for Don to place in his mind just what a gregarian was. As a small child he had seen hundreds of the little satyr-like bipeds—*faunas gregariaus veneris Smythii*—but he did not at first associate the common commercial name with the friendly, silly creatures he and his playmates, along with all other Venus colonials, had always called "move-overs" because of their chronic habit of crowding up against one, shouldering, nuzzling, sitting on one's feet, and in other ways displaying their insatiable appetite for physical affection.

Eat a baby move-over? He felt like a cannibal and for the second time in one day started to behave like a ground-hog in space. He gulped and controlled himself but could not touch another bite.

He looked back at the stage. Venusberg disappeared, giving way to a tired-eyed man who kept up a rapid fire of jokes while juggling flaming torches. Don was not amused; he let his gaze wander around the room. Three tables away a man met his eyes, then looked casually away. Don thought about it, then looked the man over carefully and decided that he recognized him. "Dr. Jefferson?"

"Yes, Don?"

"Do you happen to know a Venus dragon who calls himself 'Sir Isaac Newton'?" Don added the whistled version of the Venerian's true name.

"Don't!" the older man said sharply.

"Don't what?"

"Don't advertise your background unnecessarily, not at this time. Why do you ask about this, uh, 'Sir Isaac Newton'?" He kept his voice low with his lips barely moving.

Donald told him about the casual meeting at Gary Station. "When I got through I was dead sure that a security cop was watching me. And now that same man is sitting over there, only now he's not in uniform."

"Are you sure?"

"I think I'm sure."

"Mmm . . . you might be mistaken. Or he might simply be here in his off hours—though a security policeman should not be, not on his pay. See here—pay no further attention to him and don't speak of him again. And don't speak of that dragon, nor of anything else Venerian. Just appear to be having a good time. But pay careful attention to anything I say."

Don tried to carry out the instructions, but it was hard to keep his mind on gayety. Even when the dancers reappeared he felt himself wanting to turn and stare at the man who had dampened the party. The plate of baked gregarian was removed and Dr. Jefferson ordered something for him called a "Mount Etna." It was actually shaped like a volcano and a plume of steam came out of the tip. He dipped a spoon into it, found that it was fire and ice, assaulting his palate with conflicting sensations. He wondered how anyone could eat it. Out of politeness he cautiously tried another bite. Presently he found that he had eaten all of it and was sorry there was not more.

At the break in the stage acts Don tried to ask Dr. Jefferson what he really thought about the war scare. The doctor firmly turned the talk around to his parents' work and branched out to the past and future of the System. "Don't fret yourself about the present, son. Troubles, merely troubles—necessary preliminaries to the consolidation of the System. In five hundred years the historians will hardly notice it. There will be the Second Empire—six planets by then."

"Six? You don't honestly think we'll ever be able to do anything with Jupiter and Saturn? Oh—you mean the Jovian moons."

"No, I mean six primary planets. We'll move Pluto and Neptune in close by the fire and we'll drag Mercury back and let it cool off."

The idea of moving planets startled Don. It sounded wildly impossible, but he let it rest, since his host was a man who maintained that everything and anything was possible. "The race needs a lot of room," Dr. Jefferson went on. "After all, Mars and Venus have their own intelligent races; we can't crowd them much more without genocide—and it's not dead certain which way the genocide would work, even with the Martians. But the reconstruction of this system is just engineering—nothing to what else we'll do. Half a millennium from now there will be more Earth-humans outside this system than in it; we'll be swarming around every G-type star in this neighborhood. Do you know what I would do if I were your age, Don? I'd get me a berth in the *Pathfinder*."

Don nodded. "I'd like that." The *Pathfinder*, star ship intended for a one-way trip, had been building on, and near, Luna since before he was born. Soon she would go. All or nearly all of Don's generation had at least dreamed about leaving with her.

"Of course," added his host, "you would have to have a bride." He pointed to the stage which was again filling. "Take that blonde down there. She's a likely looking lassie—healthy at least."

Don smiled and felt worldly. "She might not hanker after pioneering. She looks happy as she is."

"Can't tell till you ask her. Here." Dr. Jefferson summoned the *maître d'hôtel;* money changed hands. Presently the blonde came to their table but did not sit down. She was a tom-tom singer and she proceeded to boom into Don's ears, with the help of the orchestra, sentiments that would have embarrassed him even if expressed privately. He ceased to feel worldly, felt quite warm in the face instead and confirmed his resolution not to take this female to the stars. Nevertheless he enjoyed it.

The stage was just clearing when the lights blinked once and the sound system again brayed forth: "Space raid warning! Space raid warning!" All lights went out.

III

Hunted

FOR AN infinitely long moment there was utter blackness and silence without even the muted whir of the blowers. Then a tiny light appeared in the middle of the stage, illuminating the features of the starring comic. He drawled in an intentionally ridiculous nasal voice, "The next sound you hear will be . . . The Tromp of Doom!" He giggled and went on briskly, "Just sit quiet, folks, and hang on to your money—some of the help are relatives of the management. This is just a drill. Anyhow, we have a hundred feet of concrete overhead—and a durn sight thicker mortgage. Now, to get you into the mood for the next act—which is mine—the next round of drinks is on the house." He leaned forward and called out, "Gertie! Drag up that stuff we couldn't unload New Year's Eve."

Don felt the tension ease around the room and he himself relaxed. He was doubly startled when a hand closed around his wrist. "*Quiet!*" whispered Dr. Jefferson into his ear.

Don let himself be led away in the darkness. The doctor apparently knew, or remembered, the layout; they got out of the room without bumping into tables and with only one unimportant brush with someone in the dark. They seemed to be going down a long hall, black as the inside of coal, then turned a corner and stopped.

"But you can't go out, sir," Don heard a voice say. Dr. Jefferson spoke quietly, his words too low to catch. Something rustled; they moved forward again, through a doorway, and turned left.

They proceeded along this tunnel—Don felt sure that it was the public tunnel just outside the restaurant though it seemed to have turned ninety degrees in the dark. Dr. Jefferson still dragged him along by the wrist without speaking. They turned again and went down steps.

There were other people about, though not many. Once

someone grabbed Don in the dark; he struck out wildly, smashed his fist into something flabby and heard a muffled grunt. The doctor merely pulled him along the faster.

The doctor stopped at last, seemed to be feeling around in the dark. There came a feminine squeal out of the blackness. The doctor drew back hastily and moved on a few feet, stopped again. "Here," he said at last. "Climb in." He pulled Don forward and placed his hand on something; Don felt around and decided that it was a parked autocab, its top open. He climbed in and Dr. Jefferson got in behind, closing the top after him. "Now we can talk," he said calmly. "Someone beat us to that first one. But we can't go anywhere until the power comes on again."

Don was suddenly aware that he was shaking with excitement. When he could trust himself to speak he said, "Doctor—is this actually an attack?"

"I doubt it mightily," the man answered. "It's almost certainly a drill—I hope. But it gave us just the opportunity that I had been looking for to get away quietly."

Don chewed this over. Jefferson went on, "What are you fretting about? The check? I have an account there."

It had not occurred to Don that they were walking out on the check. He said so and added, "You mean that security policeman I thought I recognized?"

"Unfortunately."

"But— I think I must have made a mistake. Oh, it looked like the same man, all right, but I don't see how it would have been humanly possible for him to have followed me even if he popped into the next cab. I distinctly remember that at least once my cab was the only cab on an elevator. That tears it. If it was the same cop, it was an accident; he wasn't looking for me."

"Perhaps he was looking for me."

"Huh?"

"Never mind. As to following you—Don, do you know how these autocabs work?"

"Well—in general."

"If that security cop wanted to tail you, he would not get into the next cab. He would call in and report the number of your cab. That number would be monitored in the control-net board at once. Unless you reached your destination before the monitoring started, they would read the code of your destination right out of the machine. Whereupon another security officer would be watching for your arrival. It carries on from there. When I rang for an autocab my circuit would already be monitored, and the cab that answered the ring likewise. Consequently the first cop is already seated at a table in *The Back Room* before we arrive. That was their one slip, using a man you had seen—but we can forgive that as they are overworked at present!"

"But why would they want *me?* Even if they think I'm uh, disloyal, I'm not that important."

Dr. Jefferson hesitated, then said, "Don, I don't know how long we will be able to talk. We can talk freely for the moment because they are just as limited by the power shutdown as we are. But once the power comes on we can no longer talk and I have a good deal to say. We can't talk, even here, after the power comes on."

"Why not?"

"The public isn't supposed to know, but each of these cabs has a microphone in it. The control frequency for the cab itself can carry speech modulation without interfering with the operation of the vehicle. So we are not safe once power is restored. Yes, I know; it's a shameful set up. I didn't dare talk in the restaurant, even with the orchestra playing. They could have had a shotgun mike trained on us.

"Now, listen carefully. We must locate that package I mailed to you—we *must.* I want you to deliver it to your father . . . or rather, what's in it. Point number two: you *must* catch that shuttle rocket tomorrow morning, even if the heavens fall. Point number three: you won't stay with me tonight, after all. I'm sorry but I think it is best so. Number four: when the power comes on, we will ride around for a while, talking of nothing in particular and never mentioning names. Presently I will see to it that we end up near a public common booth and you will call the *Caravansary.* If the package is there, you will leave me, go back to the Station, get your bags, then go to the hotel, register and pick up your mail. Tomorrow morning you will get your ship and leave. Don't call me. Do you understand all that?"

"Uh, I think so, sir." Don waited, then blurted out, "But why? Maybe I'm talking out of turn, but it seems to me I ought to know why we are doing this."

"What do you want to know?"

"Well . . . what's in the package?"

"You will see. You can open it, examine it, and decide for yourself. If you decide not to deliver it, that's your privilege. As for the rest—what are your political convictions, Don?"

"Why . . . that's rather hard to say, sir."

"Mmmm—mine weren't too clear at your age either. Let's put it this way: would you be willing to string along with your parents for the time being? Until you form your own?"

"Why, of course!"

"Did it seem a bit odd to you that your mother insisted that you look me up? Don't be shy—I know that a young fellow arriving in the big town doesn't look up semi-strangers through choice. Now—she must have considered it important for you to see me. Eh?"

"I guess she must have."

"Will you let it stand at that? What you don't know, you can't tell—and can't get you into trouble."

Don thought it over. The doctor's words seemed to make sense, yet it went mightily against the grain to be asked to do something mysterious without knowing all the whys and wherefors. On the other hand, had he simply received the package, he undoubtedly would have delivered it to his father without thinking much about it.

He was about to ask further questions when the lights came on and the little car started to purr. Dr. Jefferson said, "Here we go!" leaned over the board and quickly dialed a destination. The autocab moved forward. Don started to speak but the doctor shook his head.

The car threaded its way through several tunnels, down a ramp and stopped in a large underground square. Dr. Jefferson paid it off and led Don through the square and to a passenger elevator. The square was jammed and one could sense the crowd's frenetic mood resulting from the space raid alarm. They had to shove their way through a mass of people gathered around a public telescreen in the center of the square. Don was glad to get on the elevator, even though it too was packed.

Dr. Jefferson's immediate destination was another cab stand in a square several levels higher. They got into a cab and moved away; this one they rode for several minutes, then changed cabs again. Don was completely confused and could not have told whether they were north, south, high, low, east, or west. The doctor glanced at his watch as they left the last autocab and said, "We've killed enough time. Here." He indicated a communication booth near them.

Don went in and phoned the *Carvansary*. Was there any mail being held for him? No, there was not. He explained that he was not registered at the hotel; the clerk looked again. No—sorry, sir.

Don came out and told Dr. Jefferson. The doctor chewed his lip. "Son, I've made a bad error in judgment." He glanced around; there was no one near them. "And I've wasted time."

"Can I help, sir?"

"Eh? Yes, I think you can—I'm sure you can." He paused to think. "We'll go back to my apartment. We must. But we won't stay there. We'll find some other hotel—not the *Caravansary*—and I'm afraid we must work all night. Are you up to it?"

"Oh, certainly!"

"I've some 'borrowed-time' pills; they'll help. See here, Don, whatever happens, you are to catch that ship tomorrow. Understand?"

Don agreed. He intended to catch the ship in any case and could not conceive of a reason for missing it. Privately he was beginning to wonder if Dr. Jefferson were quite right in his head.

"Good. We'll walk; it's not far."

A half mile of tunnels and a descent by elevator got them there. As they turned into the tunnel in which the doctor's apartment was located, he glanced up and down it; it was empty. They crossed rapidly and the doctor let them in. Two strange men were seated in the living room.

Dr. Jefferson glanced at them, said, "Good evening, gentlemen," and turned back to his guest. "Good night, Don. It's been very pleasant seeing you and be sure to remember me to your parents." He grasped Don's hand and firmly urged him out the door.

The two men stood up. One of them said, "It took you a long time to get home, Doctor."

"I'd forgotten the appointment, gentlemen. Now, goodbye, Don—*I don't want you to be late.*"

The last remark was accompanied by increased pressure on Don's hand. He answered, "Uh—good night, Doctor. And thanks."

He turned to leave, but the man who had spoken moved quickly between him and the door. "Just a moment, please."

Dr. Jefferson answered, "Really, gentlemen, there is no reason to delay this boy. Let him go along so that we may get down to our business."

The man did not answer directly but called out, "Elkins! King!" Two more men appeared from a back room of the apartment. The man who seemed to be in charge said to them, "Take the youngster back to the bedroom. Close the door."

"Come along, buddy."

Don, who had been keeping his mouth shut and trying to sort out the confusing new developments, got angry. He had more than a suspicion that these men were security police even though they were not in uniform—but he had been brought up to believe that honest citizens had nothing to fear. "Wait a minute!" he protested. "I'm not going any place. What's the idea?"

The man who had told him to come along moved closer and took his arm. Don shook it off. The leader stopped any further action by his men with a very slight gesture. "Don Harvey——"

"Huh? Yes?"

"I could give you a number of answers to that. One of them is this—" He displayed a badge in the palm of his hand. "—but that might be faked. Or, if I cared to take time, I could satisfy you with stamped pieces of paper, all proper and legalistic and signed with important names." Don noticed that his voice was gentle and cultured.

"But it happens that I am tired and in a hurry and don't want to be bothered playing word games with young punks. So let it stand that there are four of us all armed. So—will you go quietly, or would you rather be slapped around a bit and dragged?"

Don was about to answer with school-game bravado; Dr. Jefferson cut in. "Do as they ask you, Donald!"

He closed his mouth and followed the subordinate on back. The man led him into the bedroom and closed the door. "Sit down," he said pleasantly. Don did not move. His guard came up, placed a palm against his chest and pushed. Don sat down.

The man touched a button at the bed's control panel, causing it to lift to the reading position, then lay down. He appeared to go to sleep, but every time Don looked at him the man's eyes met his. Don strained his ears, trying to hear what was going on in the front room, but he need not have bothered; the room, being a sleeping room, was fully soundproof.

So he sat there and fidgeted, trying to make sense out of preposterous things that had happened to him. He recalled almost with unbelief that it had been only this morning that Lazy and he had started out to climb Peddler's Grave. He wondered what Lazy was doing now and whether the greedy little rascal missed him.

Probably not, he admitted mournfully.

He slid a glance at the guard, while wondering whether or not, if he gathered himself together, drawing his feet as far under him as he could—

The guard shook his head. "Don't do it," he advised.

"Don't to what?"

"Don't try to jump me. You might hurry me and then you might get hurt—bad." The man appeared to go back to sleep.

Don slumped into apathy. Even if he did manage to jump this one, slug him maybe, there were three more out front. And suppose he got away from them? A strange city, where *they* had everything organized, everything under control—where would he run *to*?

Once he had come across the stable cat playing with a mouse. He had watched for a moment, fascinated even though his sympathies were with the mouse, before he had stepped forward and put the poor beastie out of its misery. The cat had never once let the mouse scamper further than pounce range. Now he was the mouse——

"Up you come!"

Don jumped to his feet, startled and having trouble placing himself. "I wish I had your easy conscience," the guard said admiringly. "It's a real gift to be able to catch forty winks any time. Come on; the boss wants you."

Don preceded him back into the living room; there was no one there but the mate of the man who had guarded him. Don turned and said, "Where is Dr. Jefferson?"

"Never mind," his guard replied. "The lieutenant hates to be kept waiting." He started on out the door.

Don hung back. The second guard casually took him by the arm; he felt a stabbing pain clear to his shoulder and went along.

Outside they had a manually-operated car larger than the robot cabs. The second guard slipped into the driver's seat; the other urged Don into the passenger compartment. There he sat down and started to turn—and found that he could not. He was unable even to raise his hands. Any attempt to move, to do anything other than sit and breathe, felt like struggling against the weight of too many blankets. "Take it easy," the guard advised. "You can pull a ligament fighting that field. And it does not do any good."

Don had to prove to himself that the man was right. Whatever the invisible bonds were, the harder he strained against them the tighter they bound him. On the other hand when he relaxed and rested he could not even feel them. "Where are you taking me?" he demanded.

"Don't you know? The city I.B.I. office, of course."

"What for? I haven't done anything!"

"In that case, you won't have to stay long."

The car pulled up inside a large garaging room; the

three got out and waited in front of a door; Don had a feeling that they were being looked over. Shortly the door opened; they went inside.

The place had the odor of bureaucracy. They went down a long corridor past endless offices filled with clerks, desks, transtypers, filing machines, whirring card sorters. A lift bounced them to another level; they went on through more corridors and stopped at an office door. "Inside," said the first guard. Don went in; the door slid shut behind him with the guards outside.

"Sit down, Don." It was the leader of the group of four, now in the uniform of security officer and seated at a horseshoe desk.

Don said, "Where is Dr. Jefferson? What did you do with him?"

"Sit down, I said." Don did not move; the lieutenant went on, "Why make it hard for yourself? You know where you are; you know that I could have you restrained in any way that suited me—some of them quite unpleasant. Will you sit down, please, and save us both trouble?"

Don sat down and immediately said, "I want to see a lawyer."

The lieutenant shook his head slowly, looking like a tired and gentle school teacher. "Young fellow, you've been reading too many romantic novels. Now if you had studied the dynamics of history instead, you would realize that the logic of legalism alternates with the logic of force in a pattern dependent on the characteristics of the culture. Each culture evokes its own basic logic. You follow me?"

Don hesitated; the other went on, "No matter. The point is, your request for a lawyer comes about two hundred years too late to be meaningful. The verbalisms lag behind the facts. Nevertheless, you shall have a lawyer—or a lollipop, whichever you prefer, after I am through questioning you. If I were you, I'd take the lollipop. More nourishing."

"I won't talk without a lawyer," Don answered firmly.

"No? I'm sorry. Don, in setting up your interview I budgeted eleven minutes for nonsense. You have used up four already—no; five. When the eleven minutes are gone and you find yourself spitting out teeth, remember that I bore you no malice. Now about this matter of whether or not you will talk; there are several ways of making a man talk and each method has its fans who swear by it. Drugs, for example—nitrous oxide, scopolamine, sodium pentothal, not to mention some of the new, more subtle, and relatively non-toxic developments. Even alcohols have been used with great success by intelligence operatives. I don't like drugs; they affect the intellect and clutter up an interview with data of no use to me. You'd be amazed at the amount of rubbish that can collect in the human brain, Don, if you had had to listen to it—as I have.

"And there is hypnosis and its many variations. There is also the artificial stimulation of an unbearable need, as with morphine addiction. Finally there is old-fashioned force—pain. Why, I know an artist—I believe he is in the building now—who can successfully question the most recalcitrant case, in minimum time and using only his bare hands. Then, of course, under that category, is the extremely ancient switch in which the force, or pain, is not applied to the person being examined but to a second person whom he cannot bear to see hurt, such as a wife, or son, or daughter. Offhand, that method would seem difficult to use on you, as your only close relatives are not on this planet." The security officer glanced at his watch and added, "Only thirty seconds of nonsense still available, Don. Shall we start?"

"Huh? Wait a minute! You used up the time; I've hardly said a word."

"I haven't time to be fair. Sorry. However," he went on, "the apparent objection to the last method does not apply in your case. During the short time you were unconscious at Dr. Jefferson's apartment we were able to determine that there actually was available a—person who meets the requirements. You will talk freely rather than let this person be hurt."

"Huh?"

"A stock pony named 'Lazy.'"

The suggestion caught him completely off guard; he was stunned by it. The man went quickly on, "If you insist, we will adjourn for three hours or so and I will have your horse shipped here. It might be interesting, as I don't believe the method has ever been used with a horse before. I understand that their ears are rather sensitive. On the other hand I feel bound to tell you that, if we go to the trouble of bringing him here, we won't send him back but will simply send him to the stockyards to be butchered. Horses are an anachronism in New Chicago, don't you think?"

Don's head was whirling too much to make a proper answer, or even to follow all of the horrid implications of the comments. Finally he burst out, "You can't! You wouldn't!"

"Time's up, Don."

Don took a deep breath, collapsed. "Go ahead," he said dully. "Ask your questions."

The lieutenant took a film spool from his desk, fed it into a projector which faced back toward him. "Your name, please."

"Donald James Harvey."

"And your Venerian name?"

Don whistled "Mist on the Waters."

"Where were you born?"

"In the *Outward Bound,* in trajectory between Luna and Ganymede." The questions went on and on. Don's inquisitor appeared to have all the answers already displayed in front of him; once or twice he had Don elaborate or corrected him on some minor point. After reviewing his entire past life he required Don to give a detailed account of the events starting with his receiving the message from his parents to take passage on the *Valkyrie* for Mars.

The only thing Don left out was Dr. Jefferson's remarks about the package. He waited nervously, expecting to be hauled up short about it. But if the security policeman knew of the package, he gave no sign of it. "Dr. Jefferson seemed to think that this so-called security operative was following you? Or him?"

"I don't know. I don't think he knew."

" 'The wicked flee when no man pursueth,' " the lieutenant quoted. "Tell me exactly what you did after you left *The Back Room.*"

"Was that man following me?" Don asked. "So help me,

I had never laid eyes on that dragon before; I was just passing the time of day, being polite."

"I'm sure you were. But I'll ask the questions. Go ahead."

"Well, we changed cabs twice—or maybe three times. I don't know just where we went; I don't know the city and was all turned around. But eventually we came back to Dr. Jefferson's apartment." He omitted mention of the call to the *Caravansary*; again, if his questioner was aware of the omission, he gave no sign of it.

The lieutenant said, "Well, that seems to bring us up to date." He switched off the projector and sat staring at nothing for some minutes. "Son, there is no doubt in my mind but what you are potentially disloyal."

"Why do you say that?"

"Never mind the guff. There's nothing in your background to make you loyal. But that is nothing to get excited about; a person in my position has to be practical. You are planning to leave for Mars tomorrow morning."

"I sure am!"

"Good. I don't see how you could have been up to much mischief at your age, isolated as you were out on that ranch. But you fell into bad company. Don't miss that ship; if you are still here tomorrow I might have to revise my opinions."

The lieutenant stood up and so did Don. "I'll certainly catch it!" Don agreed, then stopped. "Unless——"

"Unless what?" the lieutenant said sharply.

"Well, they held up my ticket for security clearance," Don blurted out.

"They did, eh? A routine matter; I'll take care of it. You can leave now. Open sky!"

Don did not make the conventional answer. The man said, "Don't be sulky. It would have been simpler to have beaten the living daylights out of you, then questioned you. But I didn't; I have a son about your age myself. And I never intended to hurt your horse—happens I like horses; I'm a country boy originally. No hard feelings?"

"Uh, I guess not."

The lieutenant put out his hand; Don found himself accepting it—he even found himself liking the man. He decided to chance one more question. "Could I say goodbye to Dr. Jefferson?"

The man's expression changed. "I'm afraid not."

"Why not? You'd be watching me, wouldn't you?"

The officer hesitated. "There's no reason why you shouldn't know. Dr. Jefferson was a man in very poor health. He got excited, suffered an attack and died of heart failure, earlier tonight."

Don simply stared. "Brace up!" the man said sharply. "It happens to all of us." He pressed a button on his desk; a guard came in and was told to take Don out. He was led out by another route but he was too bemused to notice it. Dr. Jefferson dead? It did not seem possible. A man so alive, so obviously in love with life— He was dumped out into a major public tunnel while still thinking about it.

Suddenly he recalled a phrase he had heard in class from his biology teacher, " 'In the end, all forms of death can be classed as heart failure.' " Don held up his right hand, stared at it. He would wash it as quickly as he could.

IV

The *Glory Road*

He still had things to do; he could not stand there all night. First, he supposed that he had better go back to the station and pick up his bags. He fumbled in his pouch for his claim check while he worried about just how he would get there; he still did not have hard money with which to pay off an autocab.

He failed to find the claim check. Presently he removed everything from the pouch. Everything else was there; his letter of credit; his identification card, the messages from his parents, a flat photo of Lazy, his birth certificate, odds and ends—but no claim check. He remembered putting it there.

He thought of going back into the I.B.I warren; he was

quite sure now that it must have been taken from him while he slept. Darn funny, him falling asleep like that, at such a time. Had they drugged him? He decided against going back. Not only did he not know the name of the officer who had questioned him, nor any other way of identifying him, but more importantly he would not have gone back into that place for all the baggage in Gary Station. Let it go, let it go— he'd pick up more socks and shorts before blast off!

He decided instead to go to the *Caravansary*. First he had to find out where it was; he walked slowly along, looking for someone who did not seem too busy nor too important to ask. He found him in the person of a lottery ticket vendor at the next intersection.

The vendor looked him over. "You don't want to go to that place, Mac. I can fix you up with something really good." He winked.

Don insisted that he knew what he wanted. The man shrugged. "Okay, chump. Straight ahead until you come to a square with an electric fountain in it, then take the slidewalk south. Ask anybody where to get off. What month were you born?"

"July."

"July! Boy, are you lucky—I've just got one ticket left with your horoscope combination. Here." Don had no intention at all of buying it and he thought of telling the grifter that he considered horoscopes as silly as spectacles on a cow—but he found that he had purchased it with his last coin. He pocketed the ticket, feeling foolish. The vendor said, "About half a mile on the slidewalk. Brush the hay out of your hair before you go in."

Don found the slidewalk without difficulty and discovered that it was a pay-as-you-enter express. The machine not being interested in lottery tickets he walked the catwalk alongside it to the hotel. He had no trouble finding it; its brilliantly lighted entrance spread for a hundred yards along the tunnel.

No one scurried to help him as he came in. He went to the reservation desk and asked for a room. The clerk looked him over doubtfully. "Did someone take care of your baggage, sir?"

Don explained that he had none. "Well . . . that will be twenty-two fifty, in advance. Sign here, please."

Don signed and stamped his thumb print, then got out his father's letter of credit. "Can I get this cashed?"

"How much is it?" The clerk took it, then said, "Certainly, sir. Let me have your ID, please." Don passed it over. The clerk took it and the fresh thumb print, placed both in a comparison machine. The machine beeped agreement; the clerk handed back the card. "You are you, all right." He counted out the money, deducting the room charge. "Will your baggage be along, sir?" His manner indicated that Don's social status had jumped.

"Uh, no, but there might be some mail for me." Don explained that he was going out on the *Glory Road* in the morning.

"I'll query the mail room."

The answer was no; Don looked disappointed. The clerk said, "I'll have the mail room flag your name. If anything arrives before up-ship, you'll be sure to get it—even if we have to send a messenger to the field."

"Thanks a lot."

"Not at all. Front!" As he let himself be led away Don suddenly realized that he was groggy. The big foyer clock told him that it was already tomorrow, had been for hours—in fact he was paying seven-fifty an hour, about, for the privilege of a bed, but the way he felt he would have paid more than that simply to crawl into a hole.

He did not go immediately to bed. The *Caravansary* was a luxury hotel; even its "cheap" rooms had the minimums of civilized living. He adjusted the bath for a cycling hot sitz, threw off his clothes, and let the foaming water soothe him. After a bit he changed the pattern and floated in tepid stillness.

He came to with a start and got out. Ten minutes later, dried, powdered, and tingling with massage, he stepped back into the bedroom feeling almost restored. The ranch school had been intentionally monastic, oldstyle beds and mere showers; that bath was worth the price of the room.

The delivery chute's annunciator shone green; he opened it and found three items. The first was a largish package sealed in plastic and marked "CARAVANSARY COURTESY KIT"; it contained a comb and toothbrush, a sleeping pill, a headache powder, a story film for the bed's ceiling projector, a New Chicago *News*, and a breakfast menu. The second item was a card from his roommate; the third item was a small package, a common mailing tube. The card read: *Dear Don, A package came for you on the* P.M.—*I got the Head to let me run it into Alb-Q-Q. Squinty is taking over Lazy. Must sign off; I've got to land this heap. All the best—Jack.*

Good old Jack, he said to himself, and picked up the mailing tube. He looked at the return address and realized with something of a shock that this must be the package over which Dr. Jefferson had been so much concerned, the package which apparently had led to his death. He stared at it and wondered if it could be true that a citizen could be dragged out of his own home, then so maltreated that he died.

Was the man he had had dinner with only hours ago really dead? Or had the security cop lied to him for some reason of his own?

Part of it was certainly true; he had seen them waiting to arrest the doctor—why, he himself had been arrested and threatened and questioned, and had had his baggage virtually stolen from him, for nothing! He hadn't been doing a thing, not a confounded thing, just going about his lawful business.

Suddenly he was shaking with anger. He had let himself be pushed around; he made a solemn vow never to let it happen again. He could see now that there were half a dozen places where he should have been stubborn. If he had fought right at the outset, Dr. Jefferson might be alive—if he actually were dead, he amended.

But he had let himself be bulldozed by the odds against him. He promised himself never again to pay any attention to the odds, but only to the issues.

He controlled his trembling and opened the package.

A moment later he was looking baffled. The tube contained nothing but a man's ring, a cheap plastic affair such as one might find on any souvenir counter. An old English capital "H" framed with a circle had been pressed into the face of it and the grooves filled with white enamel. It was flashy but commonplace and of no value at all to any but the childish and vulgar in taste.

Don turned it over and over, then put it aside and sorted through its wrappings. There was nothing else, not even a message, just plain white paper used to pack the ring. Don thought it over.

The ring obviously was not the cause of the excitement; it seemed to him that there were just two possibilities: first, that the security police had switched packages—if they had, there was probably nothing he could do about it—and second, if the ring were unimportant but it was the right package, then the rest of the contents of the package must be important *even though it looked like nothing but blank paper.*

The idea that he might be carrying a message in invisible ink excited him and he started thinking of ways to bring out the message. Heat? Chemical reagents? Radiation? Even as he considered it he realized regretfully that, supposing there were such a message, it was not his place to try to make it legible; he was simply to deliver it to his father.

He decided, too, that it was more likely that this was a dummy package sent along by the police. He had no way of telling what they might have forced out of Dr. Jefferson. Which reminded him that there was still one thing he could do to check up, futile as it probably would be; he stepped to the phone and asked for Dr. Jefferson's residence. True, the doctor had told him not to phone—but the circumstances had changed.

He had to wait a bit, then the screen lighted up—and he found himself staring into the face of the security police lieutenant who had grilled him. The police officer stared back. "Oh, me!" he said in a tired voice, "so you didn't believe me? Go back to bed; you have to be up in an hour or so."

Don switched off without saying anything.

So Dr. Jefferson was either dead or still in the hands of the police. Very well; he would assume that the paper came from the doctor—and he would deliver that paper in spite of all the slimily polite stormtroopers New Chicago could muster! The dodge the doctor had apparently used to fake the purpose of the paper caused him to wonder what he could do to cover up its importance. Presently he got his stylus from his pouch, smoothed out the paper, and started a letter. The paper looked enough like writing paper to make a letter on it seem reasonable—it might be writing paper in truth. He started in "Dear Mother and Dad, I got your radiogram this morning and was I excited!" He continued, simply covering space in a sprawling hand and finishing, when he was about to run out of paper, by mentioning an intention to add to the letter and have the whole thing sent off as soon as his ship was in radio range of Mars. He then folded it, tucked it into his wallet, and put the whole into his pouch.

He looked at the clock as he finished. Good heavens! He should be up in an hour; it was hardly worthwhile going to bed. But his eyes were trying to close even as he thought it; he saw that the alarm dial of the bed was graduated from "Gentle Reminder" to "Earthquake"; he picked the extreme setting and crawled in.

He was being bounced around, a blinding light was flashing in his eyes, and a siren was running up and down the scale. Don gradually became aware of himself, scrambled out of bed. Mollified, the bed ceased its uproar.

He decided against breakfast in his room for fear that he might go back to sleep, choosing instead to stumble into his clothes and seek out the hotel's coffee shop. Four cups of coffee and a solid meal later, checked out and armed with hard money for an autocab, he headed for Gary Station. At the reservation office of Interplanet Lines he asked for his ticket. A strange clerk hunted around, then said, "I don't see it. It's not with the security clearances."

This, Don thought, is the last straw. "Look around. It's bound to be there!"

"But it's— Wait a moment!" The clerk picked up a slip. "Donald James Harvey? You're to pick up your ticket in room 4012, on the mezzanine."

"Why?"

"Search me; I just work here. That's what it says."

Mystified and annoyed, Don sought out the room named. The door was plain except for a notice "Walk In"; he did . . . and found himself again facing the security lieutenant of the night before.

The officer looked up from a desk. "Get that sour look off your puss, Don," he snapped. "I haven't had much sleep either."

"What do you want of me?"

"Take off your clothes."

"Why?"

"Because we are going to search you. You didn't really think I'd let you take off without it, did you?"

Don planted his feet. "I've had just about enough pushing around," he said slowly. "If you want my clothes off, you'll have to do it."

The police officer scowled. "I could give you a couple of convincing answers to that, but I am fresh out of patience. Kelly! Arteem! Strip him."

Three minutes later Don had an incipient black eye and was nursing a damaged arm. He decided that it was not broken, after all. The lieutenant and his assistants had disappeared into a rear room with his clothing and pouch. It occurred to him that the door behind him did not seem to be locked, but he dropped the idea; making a dash for it through Gary Station in his skin did not appear to make sense.

Despite the inevitable defeat his morale was better than it had been in hours.

The lieutenant returned presently and shoved his clothes at him. "Here you are. And here's your ticket. You may want to put on clean clothes; your bags are back of the desk."

Don accepted them silently, ignored the suggestion about a change in order to save time. While he was dressing the lieutenant said suddenly, "When did you pick up that ring?"

"Forwarded to me from school."

"Let me see it."

Don took it off and flung it at him. "Keep it, you thief!"

The lieutenant caught it and said mildly, "Now, Don, it's nothing personal." He looked the ring over carefully, then said, "Catch!" Don caught it and put it back on, picked up his bags and started to leave. "Open sky," said the lieutenant.

Don ignored him.

" 'Open sky,' I said!"

Don turned again, looked him in the eye and said, "Some day I hope to meet you socially." He went on out. They had spotted the paper after all; he had noticed that it was missing when he got back his clothes and pouch.

This time he took the precaution of getting an anti-nausea shot before up-ship. After he had stood in line for that he had barely time to be weighed in before the warning signal. As he was about to get into the elevator he saw what he believed to be a familiar figure lumbering onto the cargo lift nearby—"Sir Isaac Newton." At least it looked like his passing acquaintance of the day before, though he had to admit that the difference in appearance between one dragon and another was sometimes a bit subtle for the human eye.

He refrained from whistling a greeting; the events of the past few hours had rendered him less naive and more cautious. He thought about those events as the elevator mounted up the ship's side. It was unbelievably only twenty-four hours, less in fact, since he had gotten that radio message. It seemed like a month and he himself felt aged ten years.

Bitterly he reflected that they had outwitted him after all. Whatever message lay concealed in that wrapping paper was now gone for good. Or bad.

Couch 64 in the *Glory Road* was one of a scant half dozen on the third deck; the compartment was almost empty and there were marks on the deck where other couches had been unbolted. Don found his place and strapped his bags to the rack at its foot. While he was doing so he heard a rich Cockney voice behind him; he turned and whistled a greeting.

"Sir Isaac Newton" was being cautiously introduced into the compartment from the cargo hold below with the help of about six spaceport hands. He whistled back a courteous answer while continuing to supervise the engineering feat via voder. "Easy, friends, easy does it! Now if two of you will be so kind as to place my left midships foot on the ladder, bearing in mind that I cannot see it— Wups! mind your fingers. There, I think I can make it now. Is there anything breakable in the way of my tail?"

The boss stevedore answered, "All clear, chief. Upsy-daisy!"

"If you mean what I think you mean," answered the Venerian, "then, 'On your mark; get set—GO!' " There was a crunching metallic sound, a tinkle of breaking glass, and the huge saurian scrambled up out of the hatch. Once there he turned cautiously around and settled himself in the space left vacant for him. The spaceport hands followed him and secured him to the deck with steel straps. He waggled an eye at the straw boss. "You, I take it, are the chieftain of this band?"

"I'm in charge."

The Venerian's tendrils quitted the keys of the voder, sought out a pouch by it, and removed a sheaf of paper money. He laid it on the deck and returned to the keys. "Then, sir, will you favor me by accepting this evidence of my gratitude for a difficult service well performed and distribute it among your assistants equitably and according to your customs, whatever they may be?"

The human scooped it up and shoved it into his pouch. "Sure thing, chief. Thanks."

"The honor is mine." The laborers left and the dragon turned his attention to Don, but, before they could exchange any words, the last of the compartment's human freight came down from the deck above. It was a family party; the female head thereof took one look inside and screamed.

She swarmed back up the ladder, causing a traffic jam with her descendants and spouse as she did so. The dragon swiveled two eyes in her direction while waving the others at Don. "Dear me!" he keyed. "Do you think it would help if I were to assure the lady that I have no anthropophagic tendencies?"

Don felt acutely embarrassed; he wished for some way to disown the woman as a blood sister and member of his race. "She's just a stupid fool," he answered. "Please don't pay any attention to her."

"I fear me that a merely negative approach will not suffice."

Don whistled an untranslatable dragon sound of contempt and continued with *"May her life be long and tedious."*

"Tut, tut," the dragon tapped back. "Unreasoned anguish is nonetheless real. 'To understand all is to forgive all'—one of your philosophers."

Don did not recognize the quotation and it seemed pretty extreme to him, in any case. He was sure that there were things he would never forgive no matter how well he understood them—some recent events, in fact. He was about to say so when both their attentions were arrested by sounds pouring down the open hatchway. Two and perhaps more male voices were engaged in an argument with a shrill female voice rising over them and sometimes drowning them out. It appeared (a) that she wanted to speak to the captain (b) that she had been carefully brought up and had never had to put up with such things (c) that those hideous monsters should never be allowed to come to Earth; they should be exterminated (d) that if Adolf were half a man he wouldn't just stand there and let his own wife be treated so (e) she intended to write to the company and that her family was not without influence and (f) that she *demanded* to speak to the captain.

Don wanted to say something to cover it up but he was fascinated by it. Presently the sounds moved away and died out; a ship's officer came down the hatch and looked around. "Are you comfortable?" he said to "Sir Isaac Newton."

"Quite, thank you."

He turned to Don. "Get your bags, young man, and come with me. The captain has decided to give his nibs here a compartment to himself."

"Why?" asked Don. "My ticket says couch sixty-four and I like it here."

The ship's officer scratched his chin and looked at him, then turned to the Venerian. "Is it all right with you?"

"Most certainly. I shall be honored by the young gentleman's company."

He turned back to Don. "Well . . . all right. I'd probably

have to hang you on a hook if I moved you anyway." He glanced at his watch and swore. "If I don't get a move on, we'll miss take-off and have to lay over a day." He was up and out of the compartment as he spoke.

The final warning sounded over the announcing system; a hoarse voice followed it with, "All hands! Strap down! Stand by for lift—" The order was followed by a transcription of the brassy strains of Le Compte's *Raise Ship!* Don's pulse quickened; excitement mounted in him. He felt ecstatically happy, eager to be back in space again, back where he belonged. The bad, confusing things of the past day washed out of his mind; even the ranch and Lazy grew dim.

So timed was the transcribed music that the rocket-blast effect of the final chorus merged into the real blast of the ship's tubes; the *Glory Road* stirred and lifted . . . then threw herself away into the open sky.

V

Circum-Terra

THE WEIGHT of acceleration was no worse than it had been the day before in the *Santa Fé Trail* but the drive persisted for more than five minutes, minutes that seemed like an endless hour. After they passed the speed of sound the compartment was relatively quiet. Don made a great effort and managed to turn his head a little. "Sir Isaac Newton's" great bulk was flattened to the deck, making Don think unpleasantly of a lizard crushed into a road. His eyestalks drooped like limp asparagus. He looked dead.

Don strained for breath and called out, "Are you all right?"

The Venerian did not stir. His voder instrument was covered by the sagging folds of his neck; it seemed unlikely that his tendrils could have managed the delicate touch required for its keys even had it been free. Nor did he reply in his own whistling speech.

Don wanted to go to him, but he was as immobilized by the blast weight as is the bottommost player in a football pile up. He forced his head back where it belonged so that he might breathe less painfully and waited.

When the blast died away his stomach gave one protesting flipflop, then quieted down; either the anti-nausea shot had worked or he had his space balance again—or both. Without waiting for permission from the control room he quickly unstrapped and hurried to the Venerian. He steadied himself in the air, holding with one hand to the steel bands restraining his companion.

The dragon was no longer crushed to the deckplates; only the steel hoops kept him from floating around the compartment. Behind him his giant tail waved loosely, brushing the ship's plates and knocking off paint chips.

The eyestalks were still limp and each eye filmed over. The dragon stirred only in the meaningless motion of string in water; there was nothing to show that he was alive. Don clenched a fist and pounded on the creature's flat skull. "Can you hear me? Are you all right?"

All he got out of it was a bruised hand; Sir Isaac made no response. Don hung for a moment, wondering what to do. That his acquaintance was in a bad way he felt sure, but his training in first aid did not extend to Venerian pseudo-saurians. He dug back into his childhood memories, trying to think of something.

The same ship's officer who had rearranged the berthing appeared at the forward or "upper" hatch, floating head "down." "All okay this deck?" he inquired perfunctorily and started to back out.

"No!" Don shouted. "Case of blast shock."

"Huh?" The officer swam on into the compartment and looked at the other passenger. He swore unimaginatively and looked worried. "This is beyond me; I never carried one before. How the deuce do you give artificial respiration to a thing as big as that?"

"You don't," Don told him. "His lungs are completely enclosed in his armor box."

"He looks dead. I think he's stopped breathing."

A memory floated to the top in Don's mind; he snatched it. "Got a cigarette?"

"Huh? Don't bother me! Anyhow the smoking lamp is out."

"You don't understand," Don persisted. "If you've got one, light it. You can blow smoke at his nostril plate and see whether or not he's breathing."

"Oh. Well, maybe it's a good idea." The spaceman got out a cigarette and struck it.

"But be careful," Don went on. "They can't stand nicotine. One big puff and then put it out."

"Maybe it's not such a good idea," the ship's officer objected. "Say, you sound like a Venus colonial?"

Don hesitated, then answered, "I'm a Federation citizen." It seemed like a poor time to discuss politics. He moved over to the dragon's chin, braced his feet against the deckplates and shoved, thus exposing the Venerian's nostril plate which was located under the creature's head in the folds of his neck. Don could not have managed it, save that they were in free fall, making the bulky mass weightless.

The man blew smoke at the exposed opening. It eddied forward, then some of it curled inside; the dragon was still alive.

Still very much alive. Every eyestalk sprang to rigid attention; he lifted his chin, carrying Don with it, then he sneezed. The blast struck Don where he floated loosely and turned him over and over. He threshed in the air for a moment before catching a handhold on the hatch ladder.

The ship's officer was rubbing one wrist. "The beggar clipped me," he complained. "I won't try that again soon. Well, I guess he'll be all right."

Sir Isaac whistled mournfully; Don answered him. The spaceman looked at him. "You savvy that stuff?"

"Some."

"Well, tell him to use his squawk box. I don't!"

Don said, "Sir Isaac—use your voder."

The Venerian tried to comply. His tentacles hunted around, found the keys of the artificial voice box, and touched them.

No sounds came out. The dragon turned an eye at Don and whistled a series of phrases.

"He regrets to say that its spirit has departed," Don interpreted.

The ship's officer sighed. "I wonder why I ever left the grocery business? Well, if we can get it unlatched from him, I'll see if 'Sparks' can fix it."

"Let me," said Don and squirmed into the space between the dragon's head and the deckplates. The voder case, he found, was secured to four rings riveted to the Venerian's skin plates. He could not seem to find the combination; the dragon's tendrils fluttered over his hands, moved them gently out of the way, unfastened the box, and handed it to him. He wiggled out and gave it to the man. "Looks like he kind of slept on it," he commented.

"A mess," the other agreed. "Well, tell him I'll have them fix it if possible and that I'm glad he wasn't hurt."

"Tell him yourself; he understands English."

"Eh? Oh, of course, of course." He faced the Venerian who immediately set up a long shrilling. "What's he say?"

Don listened. "He says he appreciates your good wishes but that he is sorry to have to disagree; he is unwell. He says that he urgently requires—" Don stopped and looked puzzled, then whistled the Venerian equivalent of "Say that again, please?"

Sir Isaac answered him; Don went on, "He says he's just got to have some sugar syrup."

"Huh?"

"That's what he says."

"I'll be— How much?"

There was another exchange of whistles; Don answered, "Uh, he says he needs at least a quarter of a—there isn't any word for it; it's an amount about equal to half a barrel, I'd say."

"You mean he wants half a barrel of waffle juice?"

"No, no, a quarter of that—an eighth of a barrel. What would that come to in gallons?"

"I wouldn't attempt it without a slipstick; I'm confused. I don't even know that we have any on board." Sir Isaac set up more frantic whistling. "But if we don't, I'll have the cook whop up some. Tell him to hold everything and take it easy." He scowled at the dragon, then left quite suddenly.

Don attached himself to one of the steel straps and asked, "How are you feeling now?"

The dragon replied apologetically to the effect that he needed to return to the egg for the moment. Don shut up and waited.

The captain himself showed up to attend the sick passenger. The ship, being in free trajectory for the satellite space station, would not require his presence in the control room until well past noon, New Chicago time; he was free to move around the ship. He arrived in company with the ship's doctor and followed by a man herding a metal tank.

The two conferred over the dragon, at first ignoring Don's presence. However neither of them knew the piping speech of the dragon tribe; they were forced to turn to Don. Through him Sir Isaac again insisted that he required sugar solution as a stimulant. The captain looked worried. "I've read somewhere that sugar gets them drunk the same as alcohol does us."

Don again translated for the Venerian; what he had asked for was simply a medicinal dose.

The captain turned to the medical officer. "How about it, surgeon?"

The doctor stared at the bulkhead. "Captain, this is as far outside my duties as tap dancing."

"Confound it, man, I asked for your official opinion!"

The medical officer faced him. "Very well, sir—I would say that if this passenger should die, you having refused him something he had asked for, it would look very, very bad indeed."

The captain bit his lip. "As you say, sir. But I'll be switched if I want several tons of intoxicated dragon banging around in my ship. Administer the dose."

"Me, sir?"

"You, sir."

The ship being in free fall it was quite impossible to pour out the syrup and let the Venerian lick it up, nor was he physically equipped to use the "baby bottle" drinking bladders used by humans when weightless. But that had been anticipated; the tank containing the syrup was a type used in the galley to handle soup or coffee in free fall. It had a hand pump and an attachable hose.

It was decided, Sir Isaac concurring, to place the end of the hose well down the dragon's throat. But nobody seemed to want the job. Granted that *Draco Veneris Wilsonii* is a civilized race, to stick one's head and shoulders between those rows of teeth seemed to be inviting a breach in foreign relations.

Don volunteered for the job and was sorry when they took him up on it. He trusted Sir Isaac but recalled times when Lazy had stepped on his foot quite unintentionally. He hoped that the dragon had no unfortunate involuntary reflexes; apologies are no use to a corpse.

While he kept the end of the hose firmly in place he held his breath and was glad that he had taken that anti-nausea injection. Sir Isaac did not have halitosis, as dragons go, but dragons go rather far in that direction. The job done, he was happy to back out.

Sir Isaac thanked them all, via Don, and assured them that he would now recover rapidly. He seemed to fall asleep in the midst of whistling. The ship's doctor peeled one eyestalk and shined a hand torch at it. "The stuff has hit him, I think. We'll let him be and hope for the best."

They all left. Don looked his friend over, decided that there was no point in sitting up with him, and followed them. The compartment had no view port; he wanted at least one good look at Earth while they were still close by. He found what he sought three decks forward.

They were still only fifteen thousand miles out; Don had to crowd in close to the view port to see all of Earth at one time. It was, he had to admit, a mighty pretty planet; he was a little bit sorry to be leaving it. Hanging there against velvet black and pinpoint stars, drenched in sunlight so bright it hurt your eyes, it almost took your breath away.

The sunrise line had swung far into the Pacific past Hawaii, and North America was spread out to his gaze. Storm blanketed the Pacific Northwest, but the Midwest was fairly clear and the Southwest was sharp. He could make out where New Chicago was with ease; he could see the Grand Canyon and from it he could almost figure out where the ranch had to be. He was sure that with a small telescope he could have spotted it.

He gave up his place at last. He was soaking in the pleasant melancholy of mild homesickness and the comments of some of the other passengers were beginning to annoy him—not the cheerful inanities of tourists but the know-it-all remarks of self-appointed old timers, making their second trip out. He headed back to his own compartment.

He was startled to hear his name called. He turned and the ship's officer he had met before floated up to him. He had with him Sir Isaac's voder. "You seem to be chummy with that over-educated crocodile you're bunking with; how about taking this to him?"

"Why, certainly."

"The radio officer says it needs an overhaul but at least it's working again." Don accepted it and went aft. The dragon seemed to be sleeping, then one eye waved at him and Sir Isaac whistled a salutation.

"I've got your voice box," Don told him. "Want me to fasten it on for you?"

Sir Isaac politely refused. Don handed the instrument to the fidgeting tendrils and the dragon arranged it to suit him. He then ran over the keys as a check, producing sounds like frightened ducks. Satisfied, he began to speak in English: "I am enriched by the debt you have placed upon me."

"It was nothing," Don answered. "I ran into the mate a couple of decks forward and he asked me to fetch it along."

"I do not refer to this artificial voice, but to your ready help when I was in distress and peril. Without your quick wit, your willingness to share mud with an untested stranger, and—in passing—your knowledge of the true speech, I might have lost my chance to attain the happy death."

"Shucks," Don answered, feeling somewhat pink, "it was a pleasure." He noticed that the dragon's speech was slow and somewhat slurred, as if his tentacles lacked their customary dexterity. Besides that, Sir Isaac's talk was more pedantic than ever and much more Cockney-flavored—the voder was mixing aspirates with abandon and turning the *theta* sound into "f"; Don felt sure that the Earthman who had taught him to speak must have been born in earshot of Bow Bells.

He noticed as well that his friend could not seem to make up his mind which eye he wanted to use on him. He kept waggling one after another at Don, as if seeking one which would let him focus better. Don wondered if Sir Isaac had overestimated the proper size of a medicinal dose.

"Permit me," the Venerian went on, still with ponderous dignity, "to judge the worth of the service you have done me." He changed the subject. "This word 'shucks'—I do not recognize the use you made of it. Husks of plants?"

Don struggled to explain how little and how much "shucks" could mean. The dragon thought it over and tapped out an answer. "I believe that I gain a portion of understanding. The semantic content of this word is emotional and variable, rather than orderly and descriptive. Its referent is the state of one's spirits?"

"That's it," Don said happily. "It means just what you want it to mean. It's the way you say it."

"Shucks," the dragon said experimentally. "Shucks. I seem to be getting the feel of it. A delightful word. Shucks." He went on, "The delicate nuances of speech must be learned from the living users thereof. Perhaps I may return the favor by helping you in some small wise with your already great mastery of the speech of my people? Shucks."

This confirmed Don's suspicion that his own whistling had become so villainous that it might do for popcorn vending but not for regular communication. "I certainly would appreciate a chance to brush up," he answered. "I haven't had a chance to speak 'true speech' for years—not since I was a kid. I was taught by a historian who was working with my father on the (whistled) ruins. Perhaps you know him? His name was 'Professor Charles Darwin.' " Don added the whistled or true version of the Venerian scholar's name.

"You ask me if I know (whistled)? He is my brother; his grandmother, nine times removed, and my grandmother, seven times removed, were the same egg. Shucks!" He added, "A learned person, for one so young."

Don was a bit taken aback to hear "Professor Darwin" described as "young"; as a child he had classed him and the ruins as being about the same age. He now had to remind himself that Sir Isaac might see it differently. "Say, that's nice!" he answered. "I wonder if you knew my parents? Dr. Jonas Harvey and Dr. Cynthia Harvey?"

The dragon turned all eyes on him. "You are their egg? I have not had the honor of meeting them but all civilized persons know of them and their work. I am no longer surprised at your own excellence. Shucks!"

Don felt both embarrassment and pleasure. Not knowing what to say he suggested that Sir Isaac coach him for a while in "true speech," a suggestion to which the dragon readily assented. They were still so engaged when the warning signal sounded and a voice from the control room sang out, "Strap down for acceleration! Prepare to match trajectories!"

Don placed his hands against his friend's armored sides and shoved himself back to his coach. He paused there and said, "Are you going to be all right?"

The dragon made a sound which Don construed as a hiccup, and tapped out, "I feel sure of it. This time I am fortified."

"I hope so. Say—you don't want to bung up your voder again. Want me to take care of it?"

"If you will, please."

Don went back and got it, then fastened it to his bags. He had barely time to fasten his safety belts when the first surge of acceleration hit them. It was not so bad, this time, neither as many gravities as the blast-off from Earth nor of as long duration, for they were not breaking free of Earth's crushing grip but merely adjusting trajectories—modifying the outer end of the *Glory Road*'s elliptical path to make it agree perfectly with the circular orbit of Circum-Terra, the cross-roads station in space which was their destination.

The captain gave them one long powerful shove, waited, then blasted twice more for short intervals—without, Don noted, finding it necessary to invert and blast back. He nodded approval. Good piloting!—the captain knew his vectors. The bull horn sang out, "Contact! Unstrap at will. Prepare to disembark."

Don returned the voder to Sir Isaac, then lost track of him, for the dragon again had to be taken aft to be transferred through the cargo hatch. Don whistled goodbye and went forward, towing his bags behind him, to go out through the passenger tube.

Circum-Terra was a great confused mass in the sky. It had been built, rebuilt, added to, and modified over the course of years for a dozen different purposes—weather observation station, astronomical observatory, meteor count station, television relay, guided missile control station, highvacuum strain-free physics laboratory, strain-free germ-free biological experiment station, and many other uses.

But most importantly it was a freight and passenger transfer station in space, the place where short-range winged rockets from Earth met the space liners that plied between the planets. For this purpose it had fueling tanks, machine shops, repair cages that could receive the largest liners and the smallest rockets, and a spinning, pressurized drum—"Goddard Hotel"—which provided artificial gravity and Earth atmosphere for passengers and for the permanent staff of Circum-Terra.

Goddard Hotel stuck out from the side of Circum-Terra like a cartwheel from a pile of junk. The hub on which it turned ran through its center and protruded out into space. It was to this hub that a ship would couple its passenger tube when discharging or loading humans. That done, the ship would then be warped over to a cargo port in the non-spinning major body of the station. When the *Glory Road* made contact, there were three other ships in at Circum-Terra, the *Valkyrie* in which Don Harvey had passage for Mars, the *Nautilus*, just in from Venus and in which Sir Isaac expected to return home, and the *Spring Tide*, the Luna shuttle which alternated with its sister the *Neap Tide*.

The two liners and the moon ship were already tied up to the main body of the station; the *Glory Road* warped in at the hub of the hotel and immediately began to discharge passengers. Don waited his turn and then pulled himself along by handholds, dragging his bags behind him, and soon found himself inside the hotel, but still in weightless free fall in the cylindrical hub of the Goddard.

A man in coveralls directed Don and the dozen passengers he was with to a point halfway along the hub where a large lift blocked further progress. Its circular door stood open and turned very slowly around, moving with the spinning hotel proper. "Get in," he ordered. "Mind you get your feet pointed toward the floor."

Don got in with the others and found that the inside of the car was cubical. One wall was marked in big letters: FLOOR. Don found a handhold and steadied himself so that his feet would be on the floor when weight was applied. The man got in and started the car out toward the rim.

There was no feeling of weight at first, at least not toward the "floor." Don experienced a dizzy sensation as increasing spin sloshed the liquid about in his inner ear. He knew that he had ridden this elevator before, when he was eleven and heading for Earth and school, but he had forgotten its unpleasant aspects.

Soon the elevator stopped; the floor became the floor in earnest, though with considerably less than one gravity, and the upsetting sensation ceased. The operator opened the door and shouted, "Everybody out!"

Don walked into a large inner compartment, carrying his bags. It was already crowded with more than half of the ship's passengers. Don looked around for his dragon friend, then remembered that the ship would have to be moved around to a cargo port before the Venerian could disembark. He put his bags on the floor and sat down on them.

The crowd, for some reason, seemed unquiet. Don heard one woman say, "This is preposterous! We've been here at least half an hour and no one appears to know that we're here."

A man answered, "Be patient, Martha."

" 'Patient' he says! Only one door out of the place and it locked—suppose there were a fire?"

"Well, where would you run to, dear? Nothing outside but some mighty thin vacuum."

She squealed. "Oh! We should have gone to Bermuda as I wanted to."

"As *you* wanted to?"

"Don't be petty!"

Another elevator load discharged and then another; the ship was empty. After many minutes more of grumbling, during which even Don began to wonder at the service, the only door other than the elevator door opened. Instead of a hotelman anxious to please his guests, in came three men in uniform. The two flank men were carrying mob guns cradled at their hips; the third man had only a hand pistol, still holstered. He stepped forward, planted his feet and set his fists on his hips. "Attention! Quiet, everybody."

He got it; his voice had the ring of command which is obeyed without thinking. He went on, "I am Assault Sergeant McMasters of the High Guard, Venus Republic. My commanding officer has directed me to advise you of the present situation."

There was an additional short moment of silence, then a rising mutter of surprise, alarm, disbelief, and indignation. "Pipe down!" the sergeant shouted. "Take it easy. Nobody's going to get hurt—if you behave." He went on, "The Republic has taken over this station and everybody is being cleared out. You groundhogs will be shipped back to Earth at once. Those of you who are headed home to Venus will go home—provided you pass our loyalty check. Now, let's get sorted out."

A fussy, plump man pushed his way forward. "Do you realize, sir, what you are saying? 'Venus Republic,' indeed. This is piracy!"

"Get back in line, fatty."

"You can't do this. I wish to speak to your commanding officer."

"Fatty," the sergeant said slowly, "back up before you get a boot in your belly." The man looked dumbfounded, then scuttled back into the crowd.

The sergeant continued, "Those of you going to Venus

form a queue here at the door. Have your ID's and birth certificates ready."

The passengers, up to that time a friendly group of fellow travelers, split into hostile camps. Someone shouted, "Long live the Republic!", which was followed by the beefy sound of a fist striking flesh. One of the guards hurried into the crowd and stopped the impending riot. The sergeant drew his sidearm and said in a bored voice, "No politics, please. Let's get on with the job."

Somehow a line was formed. The second in line was the man who had cheered the new nation. His nose was dripping blood but his eyes were shining. As he offered his papers to the sergeant he said, "This is a great day! I've waited all my life for it."

"Who hasn't?" the sergeant answered. "Okay—on through the door for processing. Next!"

Don was busy trying to quiet down and arrange his whirling thoughts. He was forced at last to admit that this was it, this was war, the war that he had told himself was impossible. No cities had been bombed, not yet—but this was the Fort Sumter of a new war; he was smart enough to see that. He did not have to be threatened with a boot in the belly to see what was in front of his face.

He realized with nervous shock that he had just barely gotten away in time. The *Valkyrie* might be the last ship to Mars in a long, long time. With the transfer station in the hands of the rebels it might be the last one for years.

The sergeant had not said anything about passengers for Mars as yet; Don told himself that the sergeant's first effort must naturally be to sort out the citizens of the two belligerents. He decided that the thing to do was to keep his mouth shut and wait.

There was an interruption in the queue. Don heard the sergeant say, "You're in the wrong pew, bud. You go back to Earth."

The man he was speaking to answered, "No, no! Take a look at my papers; I'm emigrating to Venus."

"You're a leetle bit late to be emigrating. The situation has changed."

"Why? Sure, I know it has changed. I declare for Venus."

The sergeant scratched his head. "This one isn't in the book. Atkinson! Pass this man on through; we'll let the lieutenant figure it out."

When he had completed the group that wanted to go to Venus the sergeant went to a speech-only wall phone. "Jim? Mac speaking, from the nursery. They got that dragon out yet? No? Well, let me know when the *Road* is back at the chute; I want to load." He turned back to the crowd. "All right, you groundhogs—there'll be a delay so I'm going to move you into another room until we're ready to send you back to Earth."

"Just a moment, Sergeant!" called out a male passenger.

"Yeah? What do you want?"

"Where do passengers for Luna wait?"

"Huh? Service discontinued. You're going back to Earth."

"Now, Sergeant, let's be reasonable. I haven't the slightest interest in politics; it does not matter to me who administers this station. But I have business on the Moon. It is *essential* that I get to the Moon. A delay would cost millions!"

The sergeant stared at him. "Now isn't that just too bad! You know, brother, I've never had as much as a thousand at one time in my life; the thought of losing millions scares me." His manner suddenly changed. "You stupid jerk, have you ever thought what a bomb would do to the roof of Tycho City? Now line up, all of you, double file."

Don listened to this with disquiet. Still, the sergeant had not said anything about Mars. He got into line, but at the very end. When the tail of the line reached the door he stopped. "Get a move on, kid," said the sergeant.

"I'm not going back to Earth," Don told him.

"Huh?"

"I'm headed for Mars in the *Valkyrie*."

"Oh, I see. You mean you were—now you're headed back to Earth in the *Glory Road*."

Don said stubbornly, "Look, mister, I've *got* to get to Mars. My parents are there; they are expecting me."

The sergeant shook his head. "Kid, I feel sorry for you. I really do. The *Valkyrie* isn't going to Mars."

"What?"

"She's being recommissioned as a cruiser of the High Guard. She's going to Venus. So I guess you had better go back to Earth. I'm sorry you won't be able to join your folks, but war is like that."

Don breathed slowly and forced himself to count up to ten. "I'm not going back to Earth. I'll wait right here until a ship does go to Mars."

The sergeant sighed. "If you do, you'll have to chin yourself on a star while you wait."

"Huh? What do you mean?"

"Because," he said slowly, "a few minutes after we blast off there will be nothing in this neighborhood but a nice, pretty radioactive cloud. Want to play a leading role in a Geiger counter?"

VI

The Sign in the Sky

DON COULD not answer. His simian ancestors, beset with perils every moment of life, might have taken it calmly; Don's soft life had not prepared him for such repeated blows. The sergeant went on, "So it had better be the *Glory Road* for you, kid. That's what your parents would want. Go back and find yourself a nice spot in the country; the cities are likely to be unhealthy for a while."

Don snapped out of it. "I'm not going back to Earth! I don't belong there; I'm not a native of Earth."

"Eh? What is your citizenship? Not that it matters; anybody who isn't a citizen of Venus goes back in the *Glory Road*."

"I'm a Federation citizen," Don answered, "but I can claim Venus citizenship."

"The Federation," the sergeant answered, "has had a slump in its stock lately. But what's this about Venus citizenship? Stow the double-talk and let's see your papers."

Don passed them over. Sergeant McMasters looked first

at his birth certificate, then stared at it. "Born in free fall! I'll be a cross-eyed pilot—say, there aren't many like you, are there?"

"I guess not."

"But just what does that make you?"

"Read on down. My mother was born on Venus. I'm Venus native born, by derivation."

"But your pop was born on Earth."

"I'm native born there, too."

"Huh? That's silly."

"That's the law."

"There are going to be some new laws. I don't know just where you fit. See here—where do you want to go? Venus or Earth?"

"I'm going to Mars," Don answered simply.

The sergeant looked at him and handed back the papers. "It beats me. And I can't get any sense out of you. I'm going to refer it on up. Come along."

He led Don down a passageway and into a small compartment which had been set up as an orderly room. Two other soldiers were there; one was using a typer, the other was just sitting. The sergeant stuck his head in and spoke to the one who was loafing. "Hey, Mike—keep an eye on this character. See that he doesn't steal the station." He turned back to Don. "Give me those papers again, kid." He took them and went away.

The soldier addressed as Mike stared at Don, then paid no further attention to him. Don put his bags down and sat on them.

After several minutes Sergeant McMasters returned but ignored Don. "Who's got the cards?" he inquired.

"I have."

"Not your readers, Mike. Where are the honest cards?" The third soldier closed the typer, reached in a drawer and pulled out a deck of cards. The three sat down at the desk and McMasters started to shuffle. He turned to Don. "Care for a friendly game, kid?"

"Uh, I guess not."

"You'll never learn any cheaper." The soldiers played cards for half an hour or so while Don kept quiet and thought. He forced himself to believe that the sergeant knew what he was talking about; he could not go to Mars in the *Valkyrie* because the *Valkyrie* was not going to Mars. He could not wait for a later ship because the station—this very room he was sitting in—was about to be blown up.

What did that leave? Earth? No! He had no relatives on Earth, none close enough to turn to. With Dr. Jefferson dead or missing he had no older friends. Perhaps he could crawl back to the ranch, tail between his legs——

No! He had outgrown that skin and shed it. The ranch school was no longer for him.

Down inside was another and stronger reason: the security police in New Chicago had made of him an alien; he would not go back because Earth was no longer his.

Hobson's choice, he told himself; it's got to be Venus. I can find people there whom I used to know—or know Dad and Mother. I'll scrounge around and find some way to get from there to Mars; that's best. His mind made up, he was almost content.

The office phone called out: "Sergeant McMasters!" The sergeant laid down his hand and went to it, pulling the privacy shield into place. Presently he switched off and turned to Don. "Well, kid, the Old Man has settled your status; you're a 'displaced person.'"

"Huh?"

"The bottom fell out for you when Venus became an independent republic. You have no citizenship anywhere. So the Old Man says to ship you back where you come from . . . back to Earth."

Don stood up and squared his shoulders. "I won't go."

"You won't, eh?" McMasters said mildly. "Well, just sit back down and be comfortable. When the time comes, we'll drag you." He started to deal the cards again.

Don did not sit down. "See here, I've changed my mind. If I can't get to Mars right away, then I'll go to Venus."

McMasters stopped and turned around. "When Commodore Higgins settles a point, it's settled. Mike, take this prima donna across and shove him in with the other groundhogs."

"But——"

Mike stood up. "Come on, you."

Don found himself shoved into a room packed with injured feelings. The Earthlings had no guards and no colonials in with them; they were giving vent freely to their opinions about events. "—outrage! We should blast every one of their settlements, level them to the ground!" "—I think we should send a committee to this commanding officer of theirs and say to him firmly—" "I *told* you we shouldn't have come!" "Negotiate? That's a sign of weakness." "Don't you realize that the war is already over? Man, this place isn't just a traffic depot; it's the main guided-missile control station. They can bomb every last city on Earth from here, like ducks on a pond!"

Don noticed the last remark, played it over in his mind, let it sink in. He was not used to thinking in terms of military tactics; up to this moment the significance of a raid on Circum-Terra had been lost on him. He had thought of it in purely personal terms, his own convenience.

Would they actually go that far? Bomb the Federation cities right off the map? Sure, the colonials had plenty to be sore about, but— Of course, it had happened like that, once in the past, but that was history; people were more civilized now. Weren't they?

"Harvey! Donald Harvey!"

Everyone turned at the call. A Venus Guardsman was standing in the compartment door, shouting his name. Don answered, "Here."

"Come along."

Don picked up his bags and followed him out into the passageway, waited while the soldier relocked the door. "Where are you taking me?"

"The C. O. wants to see you." He glanced at Don's baggage. "No need to drag that stuff."

"Uh, I guess I'd better keep it with me."

"Suit yourself. But don't take it into the C. O.'s office." He took Don down two decks where the "gravity" was appreciably greater and stopped at a door guarded by a sentry. "Here's the guy the Old Man sent for—Harvey."

"Go right on in."

Don did so. The room was large and ornate; it had been

the office of the hotel manager. Now it was occupied by a man in uniform, a man still young though his hair was shot with grey. He looked up as Don came in; Don thought he looked alert but tired. "Donald Harvey?"

"Yes, sir." Don got out his papers.

The commanding officer brushed them aside. "I've seen them. Harvey, you are a headache to me. I disposed of your case once."

Don did not answer; the other went on, "Now it appears that I must reopen it. Do you know a Venerian named—" He whistled it.

"Slightly," Don answered. "We shared a compartment in the *Glory Road*."

"Hmm. . . . I wonder if you planned it that way?"

"What? How could I?"

"It could have been arranged . . . and it would not be the first time that a young person has been used as a spy."

Don turned red. "You think I am a spy, sir?"

"No, it is just one of the possibilities I must consider. No military commander enjoys political pressure being used on him, Harvey, but they all have to yield to it. I've yielded. You aren't going back to Earth; you are going to Venus." He stood up. "But let me warn you; if you are a ringer who has been planted on me, all the dragons on Venus won't save your skin." He turned to a ship's phone, punched its keys, and waited; presently he said, "Tell him his friend is here and that I've taken care of the matter." He turned back to Don. "Take it."

Shortly Don heard a warm Cockney voice, "Don, my dear boy, are you there?"

"Yes, Sir Isaac."

The dragon shrilled relief. "When I inquired about you, I found some preposterous intention of shipping you back to that dreadful place we just quitted. I told them that a mistake had been made. I'm afraid I had to be quite firm about it. Shucks!"

"It's all fixed up now, Sir Isaac. Thanks."

"Not at all; I am still in your debt. Come to visit me when it is possible. You will, won't you?"

"Oh, sure!"

"Thank you and cheerio! Shucks."

Don turned away from the phone to find the task force commander studying him quizzically. "Do you know who your friend is?"

"Who he is?" Don whistled the Venerian name, then added, "He calls himself 'Sir Isaac Newton.' "

"That's all you know?"

"I guess so."

"Mmm—" He paused, then went on, "You might as well know what influenced me. 'Sir Isaac,' as you call him, traces his ancestry directly back to the Original Egg, placed in the mud of Venus on the day of Creation. So that's why I'm stuck with you. Orderly!"

Don let himself be led away without saying a word. Few if any Earthlings have been converted to the dominant religion of Venus; it is not a proselyting faith. But none laugh at it; all take it seriously. A terrestrial on Venus may not believe in the Divine Egg and all that that implies; he finds it more profitable—and *much* safer—to speak of it with respect.

Sir Isaac a Child of the Egg! Don felt the sheepish awe that is likely to strike even the most hard-boiled democrat when he first comes in contact with established royalty. Why, he had been talking to him, just as if he were any old dragon—say one that sold vegetables in the city market.

Shortly he began to think of it in more practical ways. If anyone could wangle a way for him to get to Mars, Sir Isaac was probably just the bird who could do it. He turned it over in his mind—he'd get home yet!

But Don did not get to see his Venerian friend at once. He was herded into the *Nautilus* along with Venus-bound passengers from the *Glory Road* and a handful of technicians from Circum-Terra whose loyalties lay with Venus rather than with Earth. By the time he discovered that Sir Isaac had been transshipped to the *Valkyrie* it was too late to do anything about it.

The flag of the task force commander, High Commodore Higgins, was shifted from Circum-Terra back to the *Nautilus*, and Higgins moved at once to carry out the rest of the coup. The storming of Circum-Terra had been managed almost without bloodshed; it had depended on timing and surprise. Now the rest of the operation must be completed before any dislocation in ship schedules would be noticed on Earth.

The *Nautilus* and the *Valkyrie* had already been prepared for their long jumps; the *Spring Tide*'s crew was removed to be sent to Earth and a crew supplied from the task force; she herself was fueled and provisioned for deep space. Although designed for the short jump to Luna, she was quite capable of making the trip to Venus. Space travel is not a matter of distance but of gravity potential levels; the jump from Circum-Terra to Venus required less expenditure of energy than did the terrible business of fighting up though Earth's field from New Chicago to Circum-Terra.

The *Spring Tide* shoved off in a leisurely, economical parabola; she would make the trip to Venus in free fall all the way. The *Valkyrie* blasted away to shape a fast, almost flat, hyperboloid orbit; she would arrive as soon or sooner than the *Nautilus*. The *Nautilus* was last to leave, for High Commodore Higgins had one more thing to do before destroying the station—a television broadcast on a globe-wide network.

All global broadcasts originated in, or were relayed through, the communications center of Circum-Terra. Since the *Nautilus* had touched in at Circum-Terra, a cosmic Trojan horse, the regular broadcasts had been allowed to continue uninterrupted. The commodore's G-6 staff officer (propaganda and nerve warfare) picked as the time for the commodore's announcement to Earth of the coup the time ordinarily given over to "*Steve Brodie Says:*", the most widely heard global news commentator. Mr. Brodie immediately followed the immensely popular "Kallikak Family" serial drama, an added advantage audience-wise.

The *Glory Road* had been allowed at last to blast off for Earth with her load of refugees but with her radios wrecked. The *Nautilus* lay off in space, a hundred miles outside, hanging in a parking orbit, waiting. Inside the space station, now utterly devoid of life, the television center continued its functions unattended. The commodore's speech had already been canned; its tape was threaded into the programmer and it would start as soon as the throb show was over.

Don watched it from a recreation lounge of the liner along with a hundred-odd other civilians. All eyes were on a big television tank set in the end of the compartment. A monitoring beam, jury-rigged for the purpose, brought the cast from Circum-Terra to the *Nautilus* and the radio watch in the ship was passing it on throughout the ship so that the passengers and crew might see and hear it.

As the day's serial episode closed, Celeste Kallikak had been arrested for suspected husband murder, Buddy Kallikak was still in the hospital and not expected to live, Father Kallikak was still missing, and Maw Kallikak was herself suspected of cheating on ration stamps—but she was facing it all bravely, serene in her knowledge that only the good die young. After the usual commercial plug ("The Only Soap with Guaranteed Vitamin Content for greater Vitacity!!") the tank faded into Steve Brodie's trademark, a rocket trail condensing into his features while a voice boomed, "Steve Brodie, with tomorrow's news *TODAY!*"

It cut suddenly, the tank went empty and a voice said, "We interrupt this broadcast to bring you a special news flash." The tank filled again, this time with the features of Commodore Higgins.

His face lacked the synthetic smile obligatory for all who speak in public telecast; his manner and voice were grim. "I am High Commodore Higgins, commanding Task Force Emancipation of the High Guard, Venus Republic. The High Guard has seized Earth's satellite station Circum-Terra. We now have all of Earth's cities utterly at our mercy."

He paused to let it sink in. Don thought it over and did not like the thought. Everybody knew that Circum-Terra carried enough A-bomb rockets to smear any force or combination of forces that could be raised to oppose the Federation. The exact number of rocket bombs carried was a military secret, variously estimated between two hundred and a thousand. A rumor had spread through the civilians in the *Nautilus* that the High Guard had found seven hundred and thirty-two bombs ready to go, with component parts for many more, plus enough deuterium and tritium to make up about a dozen Hell bombs.

Whether the rumor was true or not, Circum-Terra certainly held enough bombs to turn the Terran Federation into a radioactive abattoir. No doubt with so much under ground many inhabitants of cities would survive, but any city, once bombed, would have to be abandoned; the military effect would be the same. And many would die. How many? Forty millions? Fifty millions? Don did not know.

The commodore went on, "Mercifully we stay our hand. Earth's cities will not be bombed. The free citizens of Venus Republic have no wish to slaughter their cousins still on Terra. Our only purpose is to establish our own independence, to manage our own affairs, to throw off the crushing yoke of absentee ownership and of taxation without representation which has bled us poor.

"In so doing, in so taking our stand as free men, we call on all oppressed and impoverished nations everywhere to follow our lead, accept our help. Look up into the sky! Swimming there above you is the very station from which I now address you. The fat and stupid rulers of the Federation have made of Circum-Terra an overseer's whip. The threat of this military base in the sky has protected their empire from the just wrath of their victims for more than five score years.

"We now crush it.

"In a matter of minutes this scandal in the clean skies, this pistol pointed at the heads of men everywhere on your planet, will cease to exist. Step out of doors, watch the sky. Watch a new sun blaze briefly and know that its light is the light of Liberty inviting all Earth to free itself.

"Subject peoples of Earth, we free men of the free Republic of Venus salute you with that sign!"

The commodore continued to sit and gaze steadily into the eyes of each of his colossal audience while the heart-lifting beat of *Morning Star of Hope* followed his words. Don did not recognize the anthem of the new nation; he could not help but feel its surging promise.

Suddenly the tank went dead and at the same instant

there was a flash of light so intense that it leaked through the shuttered ports and tormented the optic nerve. Don was still shaking his head from it when over the ship's announcing system came the call: "Safe to unshutter!"

A petty officer stationed at the compartment's view port was already cranking the metal shield out of the way; Don crowded in and looked.

A second sun blazed white and swelled visibly as he watched. What on Earth would have been—so many terrible times *had been*—a climbing mushroom cloud was here in open space a perfect geometrical sphere, growing unbelievably. It swelled still larger, dropping from limelight white to silvery violet, became blotched with purple, red and flame. And still it grew, until it blanked out Earth beyond it.

At the time it was transformed into a radioactive cosmic cloud Circum-Terra had been passing over, or opposite, the North Atlantic; the swollen incandescent cloud was visible to most of the habitable portions of the globe, a burning symbol in the sky.

VII

Detour

IMMEDIATELY after the destruction of Circum-Terra the ship's warning signal howled and loudspeakers bellowed, ordering all hands to acceleration stations. The *Nautilus* blasted away, shaping her orbit for the weary trip to Venus. When she was up to speed and spin had been placed on her to permit sure footing the control room secured from blast stations. Don unstrapped and hurried to the radio room. Twice he had to argue to get past sentries.

He found the door open; everyone inside seemed busy and paid him no attention. He hesitated, then stepped inside. A long hand reached out and grabbed him by the scruff. "Hey! Where the deuce do you think you're going?"

Don answered humbly, "I just want to send a message."

"You do, eh? What do you think of that, Charlie?" His captor appealed to a soldier who was bending over a rig.

The second soldier pushed one earphone up. "Looks like a saba-*toor*. Probably an A-bomb in each pocket."

An officer wandered out of an inner room. "What goes on here?"

"Sneaked in, sir. Says he wants to send a message."

The officer looked Don up and down. "Sorry. No can do. Radio silence. No traffic outgoing."

"But," Don answered desperately, "I've just *got* to." Quickly he explained his predicament. "I've got to let them know where I am, sir."

The officer shook his head. "We couldn't raise Mars even if we were not in radio silence."

"No, sir, but you could beam Luna, for relay to Mars."

"Yes, I suppose we could—but we won't. See here, young fellow, I'm sorry about your troubles but there is no possibility, simply none at all, that the commanding officer will permit silence to be broken for any reason, even one much more important than yours. The safety of the ship comes first."

Don thought about it. "I suppose so," he agreed forlornly.

"However, I wouldn't worry too much. Your parents will find out where you are."

"Huh? I don't see how. They think I'm headed for Mars."

"No, they don't—or won't shortly. There is no secret now about what has happened; the whole system knows it. They can find out that you got as far as Circum-Terra; they can find out that the *Glory Road* did not fetch you back. By elimination, you must be on your way to Venus. I imagine that they are querying Interplanet about you right now."

The officer turned away and said, "Wilkins, paint a sign for the door saying, 'Radio Silence—No Messages Accepted.' We don't want every civilian in the ship barging in here trying to send greetings to Aunt Hattie."

Don bunked in a third-class compartment with three dozen men and a few boys. Some passengers who had paid for better accommodations complained. Don himself had had first-class passage booked—for the *Valkyrie* and Mars—but he was glad that he had not been silly enough to object when he saw the disgruntled returning with their tails between their legs. First-class accommodations, up forward, were occupied by the High Guard.

His couch was comfortable enough and a space voyage, dull under any circumstances, is less dull in the noise and gossip of a bunkroom than it is in the quiet of a first-class stateroom. During the first week out the senior surgeon announced that any who wished could avail themselves of cold-sleep. Within a day or two the bunkroom was half deserted, the missing passengers having been drugged and chilled and stowed in sleep tanks aft, there to dream away the long weeks ahead.

Don did not take cold-sleep. He listened to a bunkroom discussion, full of half facts, as to whether or not cold-sleep counted against a man's lifetime. "Look at it this way," one passenger pontificated. "You've got so long to live—right? It's built into your genes; barring accidents, you live just that long. But when they put you in the freezer, your body slows down. Your clock stops, so to speak. That time doesn't count against you. If you had eighty years coming to you, now you've got eighty years plus three months, or whatever. So I'm taking it."

"You couldn't be wronger," he was answered. "More wrong, I mean. What you've done is chop three months right out of your life. Not for me!"

"You're crazy. I'm taking it."

"Suit yourself. And another thing—" The passenger who opposed it leaned forward and spoke confidentially, so that only the entire bunkroom could hear. "They say that the boys with the bars up front question you while you are going under. You know why? Because the Commodore thinks that *spies* slipped aboard at Circum-Terra."

Don did not care which one was right. He was too much alive to relish deliberately "dying" for a time simply to save the boredom of a long trip. But the last comment startled him. Spies? Was it possible that the I.B.I. had agents right under the noses of the High Guard? Yet the I.B.I. was supposed to be able to slip in anywhere. He looked around at his fellow passengers, wondering which one might be traveling under a false identity.

He put it out of his mind—at least the I.B.I. was no longer interested in *him*.

Had Don not known that he was in the *Nautilus* headed for Venus he might well have imagined himself in the *Valkyrie* headed for Mars. The ships were of the same class and one piece of empty space looks like another. The Sun grew daily a little larger rather than smaller—but one does not look directly at the Sun, not even from Mars. The ship's routine followed the same Greenwich day kept by any liner in space; breakfast came sharp on the bell; the ship's position was announced each "noon"; the lights were dimmed at "night."

Even the presence of soldiers in the ship was not conspicuous. They kept to their own quarters forward and civilians were not allowed there except on business. The ship was forty-two days out before Don again had any reason to go forward—to get a cut finger dressed in sick bay. On his way aft he felt a hand on his shoulder and turned.

He recognized Sergeant McMasters. The sergeant was wearing the star of a master-at-arms, a ship's policeman. "What are you doing," he demanded, "skulking around here?"

Don held up his damaged digit. "I wasn't skulking; I was getting this attended to."

McMasters looked at it. "Mashed your finger, eh? Well, you're in the wrong passageway. This leads to the bomb room, not to passengers' quarters. Say, I've seen you before, haven't I?"

"Sure."

"I remember. You're the lad who thought he was going to Mars."

"I'm still going to Mars."

"So? You seem to favor the long way around—by about a hundred million miles. Speaking of the long way around, you haven't explained why I find you headed toward the bomb room."

Don felt himself getting red. "I don't know where the

bomb room is. If I'm in the wrong passage, show me the right one."

"Come with me." The sergeant led him down two decks where the spin of the ship made them slightly heavier and conducted Don into an office. "Sit down. The duty officer will be along."

Don remained standing. "I don't want to see the duty officer. I want to go back to my bunkroom."

"Sit down, I said. I remember your case. Maybe you were just turned around but could be you took the wrong turn on purpose."

Don swallowed his annoyance and sat. "No offense," said McMasters. "How about a slug of solvent?" He went to a coffee warmer and poured two cups.

Don hesitated, then accepted one. It was the Venerian bean, black and bitter and very strong. Don found himself beginning to like McMasters. The sergeant sipped his, grimaced, then said, "You must be born lucky. You ought to be a corpse by now."

"Huh?"

"You were scheduled to go back in the *Glory Road*, weren't you? Well?"

"I don't track you."

"Didn't the news filter aft? The *Glory* didn't make it."

"Huh? Crashed?"

"Hardly! The Federation groundhogs got jumpy and blasted her out of the sky. Couldn't raise her and figured she was booby-trapped, I guess. Anyhow they blasted her."

"Oh——"

"Which is why I say you were born lucky, seeing as how you were supposed to go back in her."

"But I wasn't. I'm headed for Mars."

McMasters stared at him, then laughed. "Boy, have you got a one-track mind! You're as bad as a 'move-over.' "

"Maybe so, but I'm still going to Mars."

The sergeant put down his cup. "Why don't you wise up? This war is going to last maybe ten or fifteen years. Chances are there won't be a scheduled ship to Mars in that whole time."

"Well . . . I'll make it, somehow. But why do you figure it will last so long?"

McMasters stopped to light up. "Studied any history?"

"Some."

"Remember how the American colonies got loose from England? They piddled along for eight years, fighting just now and then—yet England was so strong that she should have been able to lick the colonies any weekend. Why didn't she?"

Don did not know. "Well," McMasters answered, "you may not be a student of history, but Commodore Higgins is. He planned this strike. Ask him about any rebellion that ever happened; he'll tell you why it succeeded, or why it failed. England didn't lick the colonies because she was up to her ears in bigger wars elsewhere. The American rebellion was just a 'police action'—not important. But she couldn't give proper attention to it; after a while it got to be just too expensive and too much trouble, so England gave up and recognized their independence."

"You figure this the same way?"

"Yes—because Commodore Higgins gave it a shove in the right direction. Figured on form, the Venus Republic can't win against the Federation. Mind you, I'm just as patriotic as the next—but I can face facts. Venus hasn't a fraction of the population of the Federation, nor one per cent of its wealth. Venus *can't* win—unless the Federation is too busy to fight. Which it is, or will be soon."

Don thought about it. "I guess I'm stupid."

"Didn't you grasp the significance of blowing up Circum-Terra? In one raid the Commodore had Earth absolutely helpless. He could have bombed any or all of Terra's cities. But what good would that have done? It would simply have gotten the whole globe sore at us. As it is, we've got two-thirds of the peoples of Earth cheering for us. Not only cheering but feeling frisky and ready to rebel themselves, now that Circum-Terra isn't sitting up there in the sky, ready to launch bombs at the first sign of unrest. It will take the Federation years to pacify the associate nations—if ever. Oh, the Commodore is a sly one!" McMasters glanced up. " 'Tenshun!" he called out and got to his feet.

A lieutenant of the High Guard was in the doorway. He said, "That was a very interesting lecture, professor, but you should save it for the classroom."

"Not 'professor,' Lieutenant," McMasters said earnestly. " 'Sergeant,' if you please."

"Very well, Sergeant—but don't revert to type." He turned to Don. "Who is this and why is he loafing here?"

"Waiting for you, sir." McMasters explained the circumstances.

"I see," answered the duty officer. He said to Don, "Do you waive your right not to testify against yourself?"

Don looked puzzled. "He means," explained McMasters, "do we try the gimmick on you, or would you rather finish the trip in the brig?"

"The gimmick?"

"Lie detector."

"Oh. Go ahead. I've got nothing to hide."

"Wish I could say as much. Sit down over here." McMasters opened a cupboard, fitted electrodes to Don's head and a bladder gauge to his forearm. "Now," he said, "tell me the real reason why you were skulking around the bomb room!"

Don stuck to his story. McMasters asked more questions while the lieutenant watched a "wiggle" scope back of Don's head. Presently he said, "That's all, Sergeant. Chase him back where he belongs."

"Right, sir. Come along." They left the room together. Once out of earshot McMasters continued: "As I was saying when we were so crudely interrupted, that is why you can expect a long war. The 'status' will stay 'quo' while the Federation is busy at home with insurrections and civil disorder. From time to time they'll send a boy to do a man's job; we'll give the boy lumps and send him home. After a few years of that the Federation will decide that we are costing more than we are worth and will recognize us as a free nation. In the meantime there will be no ships running to Mars. Too bad!"

"I'll get there," Don insisted.

"You'll have to walk."

They reached "G" deck. Don looked around and said, "I

know my way from here. I must have gone down a deck too many."

"Two decks," McMasters corrected, "but I'll go with you until you are back where you belong. There is one way you might get to Mars—probably the only way."

"Huh? How? Tell me how?"

"Figure it out. There won't be any passenger runs, not till the war is over, but it is a dead cinch that both the Federation and the Republic will send task forces to Mars eventually, each trying to pre-empt the facilities there for the home team. If I were you, I'd enlist in the High Guard. Not the Middle Guard, not the Ground Forces—but the High Guard."

Don thought about it. "But I wouldn't stand much chance of getting to go along—would I?"

"Know anything about barracks politics? Get yourself a job as a clerk. If you've any skill at kissing the proper foot, a clerk's job will keep you around Main Base. You'll be close to the rumor factory and you'll know when they finally get around to sending a ship to Mars. Kiss the proper foot again and put yourself on the roster. That's the only way you are likely to get to Mars. Here's your door. Mind you don't get lost up forward again."

Don turned McMasters' words over in his mind for the next several days. He had clung stubbornly to the idea that, when he got to Venus, he would find some way to wangle passage to Mars. McMasters forced him to regroup his thoughts. It was all very well to talk about getting in some ship headed for Mars—somehow, legally or illegally, paid passenger, crew member, or stowaway. But suppose there were no ships heading for Mars? A lost dog might beat his way back to his master—but a man could not travel a single mile in empty space without a ship. A total impossibility—

But that notion of joining the High Guard? It seemed a drastic solution even if it would work and—little as Don knew about the workings of military organization—he held a dark suspicion that the sergeant had oversimplified things. Using the High Guard to get to Mars might prove as unsatisfactory as trying to hitch-hike on a Kansas twister.

On the other hand he was at the age at which the idea of military service was glamorous in itself. Had his feelings about Venus been just a touch stronger he could easily have persuaded himself that it was his duty to throw in with the colonists and sign up, whether it got him to Mars or not.

Enlisting held another attraction: it would give pattern to his life. He was beginning to feel the basic, gnawing tragedy of the wartime displaced person—the loss of roots. Man needs freedom, but few men are so strong as to be happy with complete freedom. A man needs to be part of a group, with accepted and respected relationships. Some men join foreign legions for adventure; still more swear on a bit of paper in order to acquire a framework of duties and obligations, customs and taboos, a time to work and a time to loaf, a comrade to dispute with and a sergeant to hate—in short, to *belong*.

Don was as "displaced" as any wanderer in history; he had not even a planet of his own. He was not conscious of his spiritual need—but he took to staring at the soldiers of the High Guard when he ran across them, imagining what it would be like to wear that uniform.

The *Nautilus* did not land, nor did she tie up to a space station. Instead her speed was reduced as she approached the planet so that she fell into a 2-hour, pole-to-pole parking orbit only a few hundred miles outside the silvery cloud blanket. The Venus colonies were too young, too poor, to afford the luxury of a great orbiting station in space, but a fast pole-to-pole parking orbit caused a ship to pass over every part of the spinning globe, an "orange slice" at each pass—like winding string on a ball.

A shuttle ship up from the surface could leave any spot on Venus, rendezvous with the ship in orbit, then land on its port of departure or on any other point having expended a theoretical minimum of fuel. As soon as the *Nautilus* had parked such shuttles began to swarm up to her. They were more airplane than spaceship, for, although each was sealed and pressurized to operate outside the atmosphere while making contact with orbiting spaceships, each was winged

BETWEEN PLANETS

and was powered with ramjet atmosphere engines as well
as with rocket jets. Like frogs, they were adapted to two
media.

A shuttle would be launched to catapult from the surface, her ramjets would take hold and she would climb on
her wings, reaching in the thin, cold heights of the upper
stratosphere speeds in excess of three thousand miles an
hour. There, as her ramjets failed for want of air, her rocket
jets would take over and kick her forward to orbiting speed
of around twelve thousand miles an hour and permit her
to match in with a spaceship.

A nice maneuver! It required both precise mathematical
calculation of times, orbits, fuel expenditure, and upper air
weather, and piloting virtuosity beyond mathematical calculation—but it saved pennies. Once the shuttle was loaded at
the spaceship it was necessary only to nudge it with its
rockets against the orbital direction whereupon the shuttle
would drop into a lower orbit which would eventually inter-
sect the atmosphere and let the pilot take a free ride back
to the surface, glider fashion, killing his terrible speed by
dipping ever lower into the thickening air. Here again the
pilot must be an artist, for he must both kill his momentum
and conserve it so that it would take him where he wanted
to go. A shuttle which landed out in the bush, a thousand
miles from a port, would never make another trip, even if
pilot and passengers walked away from the landing.

Don went down in the *Cyrus Buchanan*, a trim little
craft of hardly three hundred feet wingspread. From a port
Don watched her being warped in to match air locks and
noticed that the triple globes of Interplanet Lines had been
hastily and inadequately painted out on her nose and over
had been stenciled: MIDDLE GUARD—VENUS REPUB-
LIC. This defaced insignia brought the rebellion home to
him almost more than had the bombing of Circum-Terra.
Interplanet was strong as government—some said it *was* the
government. Now hardy rebels had dared to expropriate
ships of the great transport trust, paint out the proud triple
globes.

Don felt the winds of history blowing coldly around his

ears. McMasters was right; he now believed that no ship would run from here to Mars.

When his turn came he pulled himself along through the air locks and into the *Cyrus Buchanan*. The craft's steward was still in the uniform of Interplanet but the company's insignia had been removed and chevrons had been sewed to his sleeves. With this change had come a change in manner; he handled the passengers efficiently but without the paid deference of the semi-servant.

The trip down was long, tedious, and hot, as an atmosphere-braking series always is. More than an hour after touch off the airfoils first took hold; shortly Don and the other passengers felt almost full weight pressing them into the cushions, then the pilot lifted her as he decided his ship was growing too hot, let her ride out and upward in free fall. Over and over again this happened, like a stone skipping on water, a nauseating cosmic roller coaster, vastly uncomfortable.

Don did not mind. He was a spaceman again; his stomach was indifferent to surges of acceleration or even the absence thereof. At first he was excited at being back in the clouds of Venus; presently he was bored. At long, long last he was awakened by a change in motion; the craft was whistling down in its final glide, the pilot stabbing ahead with radar for his landing. Then the *Cyrus Buchanan* touched, bounced, and quivered to the rushing water under her hull. She slowed and stopped. After a considerable wait she was towed to her berth. The steward stood up and shouted, "New London! Republic of Venus! Have your papers ready."

VIII

"Foxes Have Holes and Birds of
the Air Have Nests—"

MATTHEW VIII:20

DON's immediate purpose was to ask his way to the I. T. & T. office, there to file a radiogram to his parents, but he was unable to leave at once; the passengers had to have their papers inspected and they themselves were subjected to physical examinations and questioning. Don found himself, hours later, still sitting outside the security office, waiting to be questioned. His irregular status had sent him to the end of the line.

In addition to being hungry, tired, and bored, his arms itched—they were covered from shoulders to wrists with needle pricks caused by extensive testing for immunities to the many weird diseases and funguslike infections of the second planet. Having once lived there he retained immunity to the peculiar perils of Venus—a good thing, he mused, else he would have had to waste weeks in quarantine while being inoculated. He was rubbing his arms and wondering whether or not he should kick up a fuss when the door opened and his name was called.

He went inside. An officer of the Middle Guard sat at a desk, looking at Don's papers. "Donald Harvey?"

"Yes, sir."

"Frankly, your case puzzles me. We've had no trouble identifying you; your prints check with those recorded when you were here before. But you aren't a citizen."

"Sure I am! My mother was born here."

"Mmmm—" The official drummed on his desk top. "I'm not a lawyer. I get your point, but, after all, when your mother was born, there wasn't any such nation as Venus Republic. Looks to me as if you were a test case, with precedent still to be established."

"Then where does that leave me?" Don said slowly.

"I don't know. I'm not sure you have any legal right to stay here at all."

"But I don't want to stay here! I'm just passing through."

"Eh?"

"I'm on my way to Mars."

"Oh, that! I've seen your papers—too bad. Now let's talk sense, shall we?"

"I'm going to Mars," Don repeated stubbornly.

"Sure, sure! And I'm going to heaven when I die. In the meantime you are a resident of Venus whether we like it or not. No doubt the courts will decide, eventually, whether you are a citizen as well. Mr. Harvey, I've decided to turn you loose."

"Huh?" Don was startled; it had not occurred to him that his liberty could be in question.

"Yes. You don't seem like a threat to the safety of Venus Republic and I don't fancy holding you in quarantine indefinitely. Just keep your nose clean and phone in your address after you find a place to stay. Here are your papers."

Don thanked him, picked up his bags and left quickly. Once outside, he stopped to give his arms a good scratching.

At the dock in front of the building an amphibious launch was tied up; its coxswain was lounging at the helm. Don said, "Excuse me, but I want to send a radio. Could you tell me where to go?"

"Sure. I. T. & T. Building, Buchanan Street, Main Island. Just down in the *Nautilus?*"

"That's right. How do I get there?"

"Jump in. I'll be making another trip in about five minutes. Any more passengers to come?"

"I don't think so."

"You don't sound like a fog-eater." The coxswain looked him over.

"Raised on the stuff," Don assured him, "but I've been away at school for several years."

"Just slid in under the wire, didn't you?"

"Yeah, I guess so."

"Lucky for you. No place like home, I guess." The coxswain looked happily around at the murky sky and the dark waters.

Shortly he started his engine and cast off lines. The little vessel slopped its way through narrow channels, around islands and bars barely above water. A few minutes later Don disembarked at the foot of Buchanan Street, main thoroughfare of New London, capital of the planet.

There were several people loafing around the landing dock; they looked him over. Two of them were runners for rooming houses; he shook them off and started up Buchanan Street. The street was crowded with people but was narrow, meandering, and very muddy. Two lighted signs, one on each side of the street, shone through the permanent fog. One read: ENLIST NOW!!! YOUR NATION NEEDS YOU; the other exhorted in larger letters: *Drink COCA-COLA—New London Bottling Works.*

The I. T. & T. Building turned out to be several hundred yards down the street, almost at the far side of Main Island, but it was easy to find as it was the largest building on the island. Don climbed over the coaming at the entrance and found himself in the local office of Interplanetary Telephone and Televideo Corporation. A young lady was seated behind a counter desk. "I'd like to send a radiogram," he said to her.

"That's what we're here for." She handed him a pad and stylus.

"Thanks." Don composed a message with much wrinkling of forehead, trying to make it both reassuring and informative in the fewest words. Presently he handed it in.

The girl raised her brows when she saw the address but made no comment. She counted the words, consulted a book, and said, "That'll be a hundred and eighty-seven fifty." Don counted it out, noting anxiously what a hole that made in his assets.

She glanced at the notes and pushed them back. "Are you kidding?"

"What's the matter?"

"Offering me Federation money. Trying to get me in trouble?"

"Oh." Don felt again a sick feeling at the pit of his stomach that was getting to be almost a habit. "Look—I'm just down in the *Nautilus*. I haven't had time to exchange this stuff. Can I send the message collect?"

"To *Mars?*"

"What should I do?"

"Well, there's the bank just down the street. If I were you I'd try there."

"I guess so. Thanks." He started to pick up his message; she stopped him.

"I was about to say that you can file your message if you like. You've got two weeks in which to pay for it."

"Huh? Why, thanks!"

"Don't thank me. It can't go out for a couple of weeks and you don't have to pay until we are ready to send it."

"Two weeks? Why?"

"Because Mars is right smacko back of the Sun now; it wouldn't punch through. We'll have to wait on the swing."

"Well, what's the matter with relay?"

"There's a war on—or hadn't you noticed?"

"Oh—" Don felt foolish.

"We're still accepting private messages both ways on the Terra-Venus channel—subject to paraphrase and censoring—but we couldn't guarantee that your message would be relayed from Terra to Mars. Or could you instruct someone on Earth to pay for the second transmission?"

"Uh—I'm afraid not."

"Maybe it's just as well. They might not relay it for you even if you could get someone to foot the bill. The Federation censors might kill it. So give me that traffic and I'll file it. You can pay for it later." She glanced at the message. "Looks like you sort of ran into hard luck. How old are you—" She glanced again at the form. "—Don Harvey?"

Don told her.

"Hmmm . . . you look older. I'm older than you are; I guess that makes me your grandmother. If you need any more advice, just stop in and ask Grandmother Isobel—Isobel Costello."

"Uh, thanks, Isobel."

"Not at all. Usual I. T. & T. service." She gave him a warm smile. Don left feeling somewhat confused.

The bank was near the center of the island; Don remembered having passed it. The sign on the glass read: BANK OF AMERICA & HONGKONG. Over this had been stuck strips of masking tape and under it was another sign handwritten in whitewash: *New London Trust & Investment Company*. Don went in, picked the shortest queue, and presently explained his wants. The teller hooked a thumb toward a desk back of a rail. "See him."

At the desk was seated an elderly Chinese dressed in a long black gown. As Don approached he stood up, bowed, and said, "May I help you, sir?"

Don again explained and laid his wad of bills on the banker's desk. The man looked at it without touching it. "I am so sorry——"

"What's the matter?"

"You are past the date when one may legally exchange Federation currency for money of the Republic."

"But I haven't had a chance to before! I just got in."

"I am very sorry. I do not make the regulations."

"But what am I to do?"

The banker closed his eyes, then opened them. "In this imperfect world one must have money. Have you something to offer as security?"

"Uh, I guess not. Just my clothes and these bags."

"No jewelry?"

"Well, I've got a ring but I don't suppose it's worth much."

"Let me see it."

Don took off the ring Dr. Jefferson had mailed to him and handed it over. The Chinese stuck a watchmaker's loop in his eye and examined it. "I'm afraid you are right. Not even true amber—merely plastic. Still—a symbol of security will bind the honest man quite as much as chains. I'll advance fifty credits on it."

Don took the ring back and hesitated. The ring could not possibly be worth a tenth of that sum . . . and his stomach was reminding him that flesh has its insistent demands. Still —his mother had spent at least twice that amount to make sure that this ring reached him (or the paper it had been wrapped in, he corrected himself) and Dr. Jefferson had died in a fashion somehow connected with this same bauble.

He put it back on his finger. "That wouldn't be fair. I guess I had better find a job."

"A man of pride. There is always work to be found in a new and growing city; good luck. When you have found employment come back and we can arrange an advance against your wages." The banker reached into the folds of his gown, pulled out a single credit note. "But eat first—a full belly steadies the judgment. Do me the honor of accepting this as our welcome to the newcomer."

His pride said no; his stomach said *YES!* Don took it and said, "Uh, thanks! That's awfully kind of you. I'll pay it back, first chance."

"Instead, pay it forward to some other brother who needs it." The banker touched a button on his desk, then stood up.

Don said goodbye and left.

There was a man loitering at the door of the bank. He let Don get a step or two ahead, then followed him, but Don paid him no attention, being very busy with his own worries. It was slowly beginning to grow on him that the bottom had dropped out of his world and that there might be no way to put it back together. He had lived in security all his life; he had never experienced emotionally, in his own person, the basic historical fact that mankind lives always by the skin of its teeth, sometimes winning but more often losing—and dying.

But never quitting. In a hundred yards of muddy street he began to grow up, take stock of his situation. He was more than a hundred million miles from where he meant to be. He had no way at once to let his parents know where he was, nor was it a simple matter of waiting two weeks—he was flat broke, unable to pay the high tariff.

Broke, hungry, and no place to sleep . . . no friends, not even an acquaintance—unless, he recalled, you counted "Sir Isaac," but, for all he knew, his dragon friend might be on the other side of the planet. Certainly not close enough at hand to affect the ham-and-eggs problem!

He decided to settle that problem at once by spending the note the banker had given him. He recalled a restaurant a short distance back and stopped suddenly, whereupon a man jostled him.

Don said, "Excuse me," and noted that the man was another Chinese—noted it without surprise as nearly half of the contract labor shipped in during the early days of the Venerian colonies had been Orientals. It did seem to him that the man's face was familiar—a fellow passenger in the *Nautilus?* Then he recalled that he had seen him at the dock at the foot of the street.

"My fault," the man answered. "I should look where I'm going. Sorry I bumped you." He smiled most charmingly.

"No harm done," Don replied, "but it was my fault. I suddenly decided to turn around and go back."

"Back to the bank?"

"Huh?"

"None of my business, but I saw you coming out of the bank."

"As a matter of fact," Don answered, "I wasn't going back to the bank. I'm looking for a restaurant and I remembered seeing one back there."

The man glanced at his bags. "Just get in?"

"Just down in the *Nautilus.*"

"You don't want *that* restaurant—not unless you have money to throw away. It's strictly a tourist trap."

Don thought about the single credit note in his pocket and worried. "Uh, where can a chap get a bite to eat? A good, cheap restaurant?"

The man took his arm. "I'll show you. A place down by the water, run by a cousin of mine."

"Oh, I wouldn't want to put you to any trouble."

"Not at all. I was about to refresh the inner man myself. By the way, my name is Johnny Ling."

"Glad to know you, Mr. Ling. I'm Don Harvey."

The restaurant was in a blind alley off the foot of Buchanan Street. Its sign advertised TWO WORLDS DINING ROOM—*Tables for Ladies*—WELCOME SPACEMEN. Three move-overs were hanging around the entrance, sniffing the odors and pressing their twitching noses against the screen door. Johnny Ling pushed them aside and ushered Don in.

A fat Cantonese stood behind the counter, presiding over

both range and cash register. Ling called out, "Hi, Charlie!"

The fat man answered, "Hello, Johnny," then broke into fluent cursing, mixing Cantonese, English, Portuguese, and whistle speech impartially. One of the move-overs had managed to slip in when the door was opened and was making a beeline for the pie rack, his little hooves clicking on the floor. Moving very fast despite his size the man called Charlie headed him off, took him by the ear and marched him out. Still cursing, Charlie returned to the pie rack, picked out half a pie that had seen better times and returned to the door. He tossed the pie to the fauns, who scrambled for it, bleating and whimpering.

"If you didn't feed them, Charlie," commented Ling, "they wouldn't hang around."

"You damn mind your own business!"

Several customers were eating at the counter; they paid no attention to the incident. Ling moved closer to the cook and said, "Back room empty?"

Charlie nodded and turned his back. Ling led Don through a swinging door; they ended up in a booth in the back of the building. Don sat down and picked up a menu, wondering what he could get that would stretch his one credit as far as possible. Ling took it from him. "Let me order for you. Charlie really is a number-one cook."

"But—"

"You are my guest. No, don't argue. I insist." Charlie showed up at that point, stepping silently through the booth's curtain. He and Ling exchanged remarks in a rapid singsong; he went away, returning shortly with crisp, hot egg rolls. The aroma was wonderful and Don's stomach put a stop to his protests.

The egg rolls were followed by a main dish which Don could not place. It was Chinese cooking but it certainly was not the chop suey of the trade. Don thought that he could identify Venerian vegetables out of his childhood in it but he could not be sure. Whatever it was, it was just what he needed; he began to feel a warm glow of content and ceased to be worried about anything.

While he ate he found that he was telling Ling his life history with emphasis on recent events that had landed him unexpectedly on Venus. The man was easy to talk to and it did not seem polite simply to sit, wolfing his host's food and saying nothing.

Ling sat back presently and wiped his mouth. "You've certainly had an odd time of it, Don. What are you going to do now?"

Don frowned. "I wish I knew. I've got to find a job of some sort and a place to sleep. After that I've got to scrape up, or save up, or borrow, enough money to send word to my folks. They'll be worried."

"You brought some money with you?"

"Huh? Oh, sure, but it's Federation money. I can't spend it."

"And Uncle Tom wouldn't change it for you. He's a flinty hearted old so-and-so in spite of his smiles. He's still a pawnbroker at bottom."

" 'Uncle Tom?' The banker is your uncle?"

"Eh? Oh, no, no—just a manner of speaking. He set up a hock shop here a long time ago. Prospectors would come in and pawn their Geiger counters. Next time out he'd grub-stake 'em. Pretty soon he owned half the hot pits around here and was a banker. But we still call him 'Uncle Tom.' "

Don had a vague feeling that Ling was too anxious to deny the relationship but he did not pursue the thought as it did not matter to him. Ling was continuing, "You know, Don, the bank isn't the only place where you can change Federation money."

"What do you mean?"

Ling dipped his forefinger in a puddle of water on the table top and traced out the universal credit sign. "Of course, it's the only legal place. Would that worry you?"

"Well——"

"It isn't as if there were anything wrong about changing it. It's an arbitrary law and they didn't ask you when they passed it. After all, it's your money. That's right, isn't it?"

"I suppose so."

"It's your money and you can do what you please with it. But this talk is strictly on the quiet—you understand that?"

Don didn't say anything; Ling went on, "Now just speaking hypothetically—how much Federation money do you have?"

"Uh, about five hundred credits."

"Let's see it."

Don hesitated. Ling said sharply, "Come on. Don't you trust me? After all, it's just so much waste paper."

Don got out his money. Ling looked at it and took out his wallet, started counting out bills. "Some of those big bills will be hard to move," he commented. "Suppose we say fifteen per cent." The money he laid down looked exactly like that Don had placed on the table except that each note had been overprinted with VENUS REPUBLIC.

Don did a rapid calculation. Fifteen per cent of what he had came to seventy-five credits, more or less—not even half what he needed to pay for a radiogram to Mars. He picked up his money and started putting it back into his wallet.

"What's the matter?"

"It's no use to me. I told you I needed a hundred eighty-seven fifty to pay for my radiogram."

"Well—twenty per cent. And I'm doing you a favor because you're a youngster in trouble."

Twenty per cent was still only a hundred credits. "No."

"Be reasonable! I can't move it at more than a point or two over that; I might take a loss. Commercial money draws eight per cent now, the way things are booming. This stuff has to go into hiding, losing eight per cent every year. If the war goes on very long, it's a net loss. What do you expect?"

Fiscal theory was over Don's head; he simply knew that anything less than the price of a message to Mars did not interest him. He shook his head.

Ling shrugged and gathered up his money. "It's your loss. Say, that's a handsome ring you're wearing."

"Thanks."

"How much money do you say you needed?"

Don repeated it. "You see, I've just got to get word to my family. I don't really need money for anything else; I can work."

"Mind if I look at that ring?"

Don did not want to pass it over but there seemed no way

to avoid it without being rude. Ling slipped it on; it was
quite loose on his bony finger. "Just my size. And it's got
my initial, too."

"Huh?"

"My milk name, 'Henry.' I'll tell you, Don, I'd really like
to help you out. Suppose we say twenty per cent on your
money and I'll take the ring for the balance of what you
need to send your 'gram. Okay?"

Don could not have told why he refused. But he was
beginning to dislike Ling, beginning to regret being obligated
to him for a meal. The sudden switch aroused his stubborn
streak. "It's a family keepsake," he answered. "Not for sale."

"Eh? You're in no position to be sentimental. The ring is
worth more here than it is on Earth—but I'm still offering you
much more than it's worth. Don't be a fool!"

"I know you are," Don answered, "and I don't understand
why you are. In any case the ring is not for sale. Give it
back to me."

"And suppose I don't?"

Don took a deep breath. "Why then," he said slowly, "I
suppose I'll have to fight you for it."

Ling looked at him for a moment, then took off the ring
and dropped it on the table. He then walked out of the
booth without saying anything more.

Don stared after him and tried to figure it out. He was
still wondering when the curtain was pushed aside and the
restaurant keeper came in. He dropped a chit on the table.
"One and six," he said stolidly.

"Didn't Mr. Ling pay for it? He invited me to have dinner with him."

"One and six," Charlie repeated. "You ate. You pay."

Don stood up. "Where do you wash dishes around here?
I might as well get started."

IX

"Bone" Money

BEFORE the evening was over the job of washing dishes for his dinner developed into a fixed arrangement. The salary was small—Don calculated that it would take him roughly forever to save enough money to send a radiogram to his parents—but it included three meals a day of Charlie's superlative cooking. Charlie himself seemed a very decent sort under his gruffness. He expressed a complicated and most disparaging opinion of Johnny Ling, using the same highly spiced *lingua franca* that he had used on the move-overs. He also denied any relationship to Ling while attributing to Ling other relationships which were on the face of them improbable.

After the last customer was gone and the last dish dried Charlie made up a pallet for Don on the floor of the back room in which Don had dined. As Don undressed and crawled into bed he remembered that he should have phoned the space port security office and told them his address. Tomorrow would do, he thought sleepily; anyhow the restaurant had no phone.

He woke up in darkness with a feeling of oppression. For a terrified moment he thought someone was holding him down and trying to rob him. As he came wider awake he realized where he was and what was causing the oppressed feeling—move-overs. There were two of them in bed with him; one was snuggled up to his back and was holding onto his shoulders; the other was cradled in his lap, spoon-fashion. Both were snoring gently. Someone had undoubtedly left a door open for a moment and they had sneaked in.

Don chuckled to himself. It was impossible to be angry with the affectionate little creatures. He scratched the one in front of him between its horns and said, "Look, kids, this is *my* bed. Now get out of here before I get tough."

They both bleated and snuggled closer. Don got up,

got each of them by an ear and evicted them through the curtain. "Now stay out!"

They were back in bed before he was.

Don thought about it and gave up. The back room had no door that could be closed. As for chucking them outside the building, the place was dark and still strange to him and he was not sure of the locations of light switches. Nor did he want to wake Charlie. After all there was no harm in bedding down with a move-over; they were cleanly little things, no worse than having a dog curl up against one—better, for dogs harbor fleas. "Move over," he ordered, unintentionally renaming them, "and give me some room."

He did not go at once to sleep; the dream that had awakened him still troubled him. He sat up, fumbled in the dark, and found his money, which he tucked under him. He then remembered the ring, and, feeling somewhat foolish, he pulled on a sock and stuffed the ring far down into the sock.

Presently all three of them were snoring.

He was awakened by a frightened bleating in his ear. The next few moments were quite confused. He sat up, whispered, "Pipe down!" and started to smack his bedmate, when he felt his wrist grasped by a hand—not the thumbless little paw of a move-over, but a human hand.

He kicked out and connected with something. There was a grunt, more anguished bleating, and the click-click-click of little hooves on bare floor. He kicked again and almost broke his toe; the hand let go.

He backed away while getting to his feet. There were sounds of struggle near him and loud bleating. The sounds died down while he was still trying to peer through the darkness to find out what was happening. Then a light came on blindingly and he saw Charlie standing in the door, dressed in a wrap-around and a big, shiny cleaver. "What's the matter with you?" Charlie demanded.

Don did his best to explain but move-overs, dreams, and clutching hands in the dark were badly mixed together. "You eat too much late at night," Charlie decided. Nevertheless he checked the place, with Don trailing after.

When he came to a window with a broken hasp he did not say anything but went at once to the cash register and the lock box. Neither seemed to have been disturbed. Charlie nailed up the broken catch, shoved the move-overs back into the night, and said, "Go to sleep," to Don. He returned to his own room.

Don tried to do so but it was some time before he could quiet down. Both his money and the ring were still at hand. He put the ring back on his finger and went to sleep with his fist clenched.

Next morning Don had plenty of time to think as he coped with an unending stack of dirty dishes. The ring was on his mind. He was not wearing it; not only did he wish to avoid plunging it repeatedly into hot water but also was now reluctant to display it.

Could it be possible that the thief was after the ring rather than his money? It seemed impossible—a half-credit piece of souvenir counter junk! Or perhaps five credits, he corrected himself, here on Venus where every important item was expensive. Ten at the outside.

But he was beginning to wonder; too many people had taken an interest in it. He reviewed in his mind how he had come by it. On the face of it, Dr. Jefferson had risked death—had died—to make sure that the ring went to Mars. But that was preposterous and because it was he had concluded by what seemed to be strict logic that it must have been the paper in which the ring was wrapped that must reach his parents on Mars. That conclusion had been confirmed when the I.B.I. had searched him and confiscated the wrapping paper.

Suppose he did assume the wild possibility that it was the ring itself that was important? Even so, how could anyone here on Venus be looking for that ring? He had just landed; he had not even known that he was coming to Venus.

He might have thought of several ways that that news could have gone on before him, but he did not. Moreover, he found it difficult to imagine why anyone would take any special pains on his account.

But he had one quality in a high degree; he was stubborn. He swore a mighty oath into the dishwater that he and the ring, together, would travel to Mars and that he would deliver it to his father as Dr. Jefferson had asked him to.

Business slacked off a little in the middle of the afternoon; Don got caught up. He dried his hands and said to Charlie, "I want to go uptown for a while."

"What's a matter? You lazy?"

"We work tonight, don't we?"

"Sure we do. You think this is a tea room?"

"Okay, I work mornings and evenings—so I take a little time off in the afternoon. You've got enough clean dishes to last you for hours."

Charlie shrugged and turned his back. Don left.

He picked his way through the mud and the crowd back up the street to the I. T. & T. Building. The outer room held several customers but most of them were using the automatic phones or waiting outside the booths for a chance to do so. Isobel Costello was back of the desk and did not seem too busy, although she was chatting with a soldier. Don went to the far end of the desk and waited for her to be free.

Presently she brushed off the enterprising soldier and came to him. "Well, if it isn't my problem child! How are you making out, son? Get your money changed?"

"No, the bank wouldn't take it. I guess you had better give me back my 'gram."

"No hurry; Mars is still in conjunction. Maybe you'll strike it rich."

Don laughed ruefully. "Not likely!" He told her what he was doing and where.

She nodded. "You could do worse. Old Charlie is all right. But that's a rough part of town, Don. Be careful, especially after dark."

"I will be. Isobel, would you do me a favor?"

"If it's not impossible, illegal, or scandalous—yes."

Don fished the ring out of his pocket. "Would you take care of this for me? Keep it safe until I want it back?"

She took it, held it up to look at it. "Careful!" Don urged. "Keep it out of sight."

"Huh?"

"I don't want anyone to know you have it. Get it out of sight."

"Well—" She turned away; when she turned back the ring was gone. "What's the mystery, Don?"

"I wish I knew."

"Huh?"

"I can't tell you any more than that. I just want to keep that ring safe. Somebody is trying to get it away from me."

"But— Look, does it belong to you?"

"Yes. That's all I can tell you."

She searched his face. "All right, Don. I'll take care of it."

"Thanks."

"No trouble—I hope. Look—stop in again soon. I want you to meet the manager."

"Okay, I will."

She turned away to take care of a customer. Don waited around until a phone booth was free, then reported his address to the security office at the space port. That done, he returned to his dishes.

Around midnight, hundreds of dishes later, Charlie turned away the last customer and locked the front door. Together they ate a meal there had been no time for earlier, one with chopsticks, one with fork. Don found himself almost too tired to eat. "Charlie," he asked, "how did you run this place with no help?"

"Had two helpers. Both joined up. Boys don't want to work these days; all they think about is playing soldier."

"So I'm filling two jobs, eh? Better hire another boy, or I might join up, too."

"Work is good for you."

"Maybe. You certainly take your own advice; I've never seen anybody work as hard as you do."

Charlie leaned back and rolled a cigarette of the shaggy native "crazy weed." "While I work I think about how someday I go home. A little garden with a wall around it. A little bird to sing to me." He waved his hand through choking smoke at the dreary walls of the restaurant. "While I cook, I don't see this. I see my little garden."

"Oh."

"I save money to go home." He puffed furiously. "I go home—or my bones will."

Don understood him; he had heard of "bone money" in his childhood. All the immigrant Chinese planned to go home; too often it was only a package of bones that made the trip. The younger, Venus-born Chinese laughed at the idea; to them Venus was home and China only a much-gummed tale.

He decided to tell Charlie his own troubles and did so, omitting any mention of the ring and all connected with it. "So you see, I'm just as anxious to get to Mars as you are to go home to China."

"Mars is a long way off."

"Yes—but I've got to get there."

Charlie finished his cigarette and stood up. "You stick with Charlie. Work hard and I cut you in on the profits. Someday this war nonsense will be over—then we both go." He turned to go. "G'night."

"Good night." This time Don checked personally to see that no move-overs had managed to sneak in, then retired to his cubbyhole. He was asleep almost at once, to dream of climbing endless mountain ranges of dishes, with Mars somewhere beyond.

Don was lucky to have a cubbyhole in a cheap restaurant as a place to sleep; the city was bursting at its seams. Even before the political crisis which had turned it into the capital of a new nation New London had been a busy place, market place for a million square miles of back country and principal space port of the planet. The *de facto* embargo on interplanetary shipping resulting from the outbreak of war with the mother planet might eventually starve the fat off the city but as yet the only effect had been to spill into the town grounded spacemen who prowled the streets and sampled what diversions the town offered.

The spacemen were hardly noticed; much more numerous were the politicians. On Governor's Island, separated from Main Island by a stagnant creek, the Estates General of the new republic was in session; nearby, in what had been the gubernatorial mansion, the Executive General, his chief of State, and the departmental ministers bickered with each other over office space and clerical help. Already a budding bureaucracy was spilling over onto Main Island, South Island, East Spit, and Tombstone Island, vying with each other for buildings and sending rents sky high. In the wake of the statesmen and elected officials—and much more numerous—were the small fry and hangers-on of government, clerks who worked and special assistants who did not, world savers, men with Messages, lobbyists for and lobbyists against, men who claimed to speak for the native dragons but had never gotten around to learning whistle speech, and dragons who were quite capable of speaking on their own behalf—and did.

Nevertheless Governor's Island did not sink under the load.

North of the city on Buchanan Island another city was burgeoning—training camps for the Middle Guard and the Ground Forces. It was protested bitterly in the Estates that the presence of training grounds at the national capital was an invitation to national suicide, as one H-bomb could wipe out both the government and most of the armed forces of Venus—nevertheless nothing had been done about it. It was argued that the men had to have some place for recreation; if the training grounds were moved out into the trackless bush, the men would desert and go back to their farms and mines.

Many *had* deserted. In the meantime New London swarmed with soldiery. The Two Worlds Dining Room was jammed from morning until night. Old Charlie left the range only to tend the cash register; Don's hands were raw from hot water and detergent. Between times he stoked the water boiler back of the shack, using oily *Chika* logs hauled in by a dragon known as "Daisy" (but male despite the chosen name). Electric water heating would have been cheaper; electric power was an almost-costless by-product of the atomic pile west of the city—but the equipment to use electric power was very expensive and almost unobtainable.

New London was full of such frontier contrasts. Its muddy, unpaved streets were lighted, here and there, by atomic power. Rocket-powered sky shuttles connected it with other human settlements but inside its own boundaries transportation was limited to shank's ponies and to the gondolas that served in lieu of taxis and tubes—some of these were powered, more moved by human muscle.

New London was ugly, uncomfortable, and unfinished, but it was stimulating. Don liked the gusty, brawling drive of the place, liked it much better than the hothouse lushness of New Chicago. It was as alive as a basketful of puppies, as vital as a punch in the jaw. There was a feeling in the air of new things about to happen, new hopes, new problems—

After a week in the restaurant Don felt almost as if he had been there all his life. Furthermore he was not unhappy at it. Oh, to be sure, the work was hard, and he still was determined to get to Mars—eventually—but in the meantime he slept well, ate well, and had his hands busy . . . and there were always the customers to talk and argue with—spacemen, guardsmen, small-time politicians who could not afford the better restaurants. The place was a political debating club, city news desk, and rumor mill; the gossip swapped over Charlie's food was often tomorrow's headline in the New London *Times*.

Don kept up the precedent of a midafternoon break, even when he had no business to transact. If Isobel was not too busy, he would take her across the street for a coke; she was, as yet, his only friend outside the restaurant. On one such occasion she said, "No—come on inside. I want you to meet the manager."

"Eh?"

"About your 'gram."

"Oh, yes—I'd been meaning to, Isobel, but there's no point in it yet. I haven't got the money. I'm going to wait another week and hit Old Charlie for a loan. He can't replace me very easily; I think he'll come across to keep me in durance vile."

"That's no good—you ought to get a better job as soon as you can. Come on."

She opened the gate in the counter desk and led him into an office in the rear where she introduced him to a worried-looking middle-aged man. "This is Don Harvey, the young man I was telling you about."

The older man shook hands. "Oh, yes—something about a message to Mars, I think my daughter said."

Don turned to Isobel. " 'Daughter'? You didn't tell me the manager was your father."

"You didn't ask me."

"But— Never mind. Glad to know you, sir."

"And you. Now about that message——"

"I don't know why Isobel brought me in here. I can't pay for it. All I have is Federation money."

Mr. Costello examined his nails and looked troubled. "Mr. Harvey, under the rules I am supposed to require cash payment for interplanetary traffic. I'd like to accept your Federation notes. But I can't; it's against the law." He stared at the ceiling. "Of course there is a black market in Federation money——"

Don grinned ruefully. "So I found out. But fifteen, or even twenty per cent, is too low a rate. I still couldn't pay for my 'gram."

"Twenty per cent! The going rate is sixty per cent."

"It is? I guess I must have looked like a sucker."

"Never mind. I was not going to suggest that you go to the black market. In the first place—Mr. Harvey, I am in the odd position of representing a Federation corporation which has not been expropriated, but I am loyal to the Republic. If you walked out of here and returned shortly with money of the Republic instead of Federation notes, I would simply call the police."

"Oh, Daddy, you wouldn't!"

"Quiet, Isobel. In the second place, it's not good for a young man to have such dealings." He paused. "But perhaps we can work something out. Your father would pay for this message, would he not?"

"Oh, certainly!"

"But I can't send it collect. Very well; write a draft on your father for the amount; I'll accept it as payment."

Instead of answering at once, Don thought about it. It seemed to be the same thing as sending a message collect—which he was willing to do—but running up debts in his father's name and without his knowledge stuck in his craw. "See here, Mr. Costello, you couldn't cash such a draft any time soon in any case: why don't I just give you an I.O.U. and pay it back as quickly as possible? Isn't that better?"

"Yes and no. Your personal note is simply a case of letting you have interplanetary service on credit—which is what the rules forbid. On the other hand, a draft on your father is commercial paper, equivalent to cash even if I can't cash it right away. A space lawyer's difference, granted—but it's the difference between what I can do and can't do with the corporation's affairs."

"Thanks," Don said slowly, "but I think I'll wait a while. I may be able to borrow the money elsewhere."

Mr. Costello looked from Don to Isobel, shrugged helplessly. "Oh, give me your I.O.U." he said snappishly. "Make it out to me, not to the company. You can pay me when you can." He looked again at his daughter who was smiling approval.

Don made out the note. When Isobel and he were out of earshot of her father, Don said, "That was a mighty generous thing for your father to do."

"Pooh!" she answered. "It just goes to show how far a doting father will go not to crimp his daughter's chances."

"Huh? What do you mean?"

She grinned at him. "Nothing. Nothing at all. Grandmother Isobel was pulling your leg. Don't take me seriously."

He grinned back. "Then where should I take you? Across to the Dutchman's for a coke?"

"You've talked me into it."

When he got back to the restaurant he found, in addition to the inevitable stack of dishes, a heated discussion about the draft bill pending in the Estates General. He pricked up his ears; if conscription came, he was sure fodder for it and he wanted to beat them to it by enlisting in the High Guard. McMasters' advice about the "only way to get to Mars" stuck in his mind.

Most of the opinions seemed to favor a draft, nor could Don argue against it; it seemed reasonable to him even though he would be caught in it. One quiet little man heard the others out, then cleared his throat. "There will be no draft," he announced.

The last speaker, a co-pilot still wearing the triple globes on his collar, answered, "Huh? What do you know about it, Shorty?"

"Quite a bit. Let me introduce myself—Senator Ollendorf of CuiCui Province. In the first place we don't need a draft; the nature of our dispute with the Federation is not such as to employ a large army. Secondly, our people are not of the temperament to put up with it. By the drastic process of selective immigration we have here on Venus a nation of hardy individualists, almost anarchists. They don't take to forced service. Thirdly, the taxpayers will not support a mass army; we have more volunteers now than we can find money to pay for. Lastly, my colleagues and I are going to vote it down about three to one."

"Shorty," complained the co-pilot, "why did you bother with the first three reasons?"

"Just practicing the speech I mean to make tomorrow," apologized the Senator. "Now, sir, since you are so strong for the draft, pray tell why you haven't joined the High Guard? You are obviously qualified."

"Well, I'll tell you, just like you told me. First or firstly, I'm not a colonial, so it's not my war. Secondly, this is my first vacation since the time they grounded the *Comet*-class ships. And thirdly, I joined up yesterday and I'm drinking up my bounty money before reporting in. Does that satisfy you?"

"Completely, sir! May I buy you a drink?"

"Old Charlie doesn't serve anything but coffee—you ought to know that. Here, have a mug and tell us what's cooking over on Governor's Island. Give us the inside data."

Don kept his ears open and his mouth (usually) shut. Among other things he learned why the "war" was producing no military action—other than the destruction of Circum-Terra. It was not alone that a distance varying from about thirty million to better than one hundred fifty million miles was, to say the least, awkwardly inconvenient for military communications; more important was the fear of retaliation which seemed to have produced a stalemate.

A sergeant technician of the Middle Guard outlined it to anyone who would listen: "Now they want to keep everybody up half the night with space raid alerts. Malarky!

Terra won't attack—the big boys that run the Federation know better. The war's over."

"Why do you figure they won't attack?" Don asked. "Seems to me we're sitting ducks here."

"Sure we are. One bomb and they blow this mudhole out of the swamp. Same for Buchanan. Same for CuiCui Town. What good does that do them?"

"I don't know, but I don't relish being A-bombed."

"You won't be! Use your head. They knock out a few shopkeepers and a lot of politicians—and they don't touch the back country. Venus Republic is as strong as ever—because those three spots are the only targets fit to bomb on this whole fogbound world. Then what happens?"

"It's your story; you tell me."

"A dose of reprisal, that's what—with all those bombs Comdore Higgins snagged out of Circum-Terra. We've got some of their fastest ships and we'd have the juiciest targets in history to shoot at. Everything from Detroit to Bolivar—steel mills, power plants, factories. They won't risk pulling our nose when they know we're all set to kick them in the belly. Let's be logical!" The sergeant set down his cup and looked around triumphantly.

A quiet man at the end of the counter had been listening. Now he said softly, "Yes—but how do you know that the strong men in the Federation will use logic?"

The sergeant looked surprised. "Huh? Oh, come off it! The war's over, I tell you. We ought to go home. I've got forty acres of the best rice paddies on the planet; somebody's got to get the crop in. Instead I'm sitting around here, playing space raid drill. The government ought to do something."

X

"While I Was Musing the Fire Burned"

PSALM XXXIX:3

THE GOVERNMENT did do something; the draft act was passed the next day. Don heard about it at noon; as soon as the lunch hour rush was over he dried his hands and went uptown to the recruiting station. There was a queue in front of it; he joined its tail and waited.

Over an hour later he found himself facing a harried-looking warrant officer seated at a table. He shoved a form at Don. "Print your name. Sign at the bottom and thumb it. Then hold up your right hand."

"Just a minute," Don answered. "I want to enlist in the High Guard. This forms reads for the Ground Forces."

The officer swore mildly. "Everybody wants the High Guard. Listen, son, the quota for the High Guard was filled at nine o'clock this morning—now I'm not even accepting them for the waiting list."

"But I don't want the Ground Forces. I'm—I'm a space-man."

The man swore again, not so mildly. "You don't look it. You last-minute patriots make me sick—trying to join the sky boys so you won't have to soldier in the mud. Go on home; when we want you we'll send for you—and it won't be for the High Guard. You'll be a duckfoot and like it."

"But——"

"Get out, I said."

Don got. When he reached the restaurant Old Charlie looked at the clock, then at him. "You soldier boy now?"

"They wouldn't have me."

"Good thing. Get me up some cups."

He had time to think about it while bending over suds. Although not inclined to grieve over spilt milk Don could see now that Sergeant McMasters' advice had been shrewd; he had missed what was probably his only chance (slim as it might have been) to get to Mars. It seemed a vacuum-tight certainty that he would spend the war (months? years?) as a duckfoot in the Ground Forces, getting no nearer to Mars than opposition distance—say sixty, seventy million miles. Hardly shouting distance.

He thought about the possibility of claiming exemption on the basis of Terran citizenship—but discarded it at once. He had already claimed the right to come here as a citizen of Venus; blowing hot and cold from the same mouth did not suit him. His sympathies lay with Venus anyhow, no matter what the lawyers eventually decided about his nationality.

More than that, even if he could stomach making such a claim, he could not see himself behind wire in an enemy alien camp. There was such a camp, he knew, over on East Spit. Sit out the war there and let Isobel bring him packages on Sunday afternoons?

Don't kid yourself, Don, my boy—Isobel was fiercely patriotic; she'd drop you like a mud louse.

"What can't be cured must be endured"—Confucius or somebody. He was in it and that was that—he didn't feel too upset about it; the Federation didn't have any business throwing its weight around on Venus anyhow. Whose planet was it?

He was most anxious to get in touch with his parents and to let them know he had Dr. Jefferson's ring, even if he couldn't deliver it right away. He would have to get up to the I. T. & T. office and check—there might be communication today. Charlie ought to have a phone in this dump.

He remembered that he had one possible resource that he had not exploited—"Sir Isaac." He had sincerely intended to get in touch with his dragon friend as soon as he landed, but it had not proved to be easy. "Sir Isaac" had not landed at New London, nor had he been able to find out from the local office where he had landed. Probably at CuiCui Town or at Buchanan—or, possibly, since "Sir Isaac" was a V.I.P., the Middle Guard might have accommodated him with a special landing. He might be anywhere on a planet with more land surface than Earth.

Of course, such an important personage could be traced down—but the first step would be to consult the Office of Aborigine Affairs over on Governor's Island. That meant a two-hour trip, what with a gondola ride both ways and the red tape he was sure to run into. He told himself that he just hadn't had time.

But now he must take time. "Sir Isaac" might be able to get him assigned, or transferred, to the High Guard, quotas or no. The government was extremely anxious to keep the dragons happy and friendly to the new regime. Mankind remained on Venus at the sufferance of the dragons; the politicians knew that.

He felt a little bit sheepish about resorting to political influence—but there were times when nothing else would work.

"Charlie!"

"Huh?"

"Go easy on the spoons; I've got to go uptown again."

Charlie grunted grumpily; Don hung up his apron and left. Isobel was not on the desk at I. T. & T.; Don sent in his name via the clerk on duty and got in to see her father. Mr. Costello looked up as he came in and said, "I'm glad you came in, Mr. Harvey. I wanted to see you."

"My message got through?"

"No, I wanted to give you back your note."

"Huh? What's the matter?"

"I haven't been able to send your message and I don't know when I shall be able to send it. If it turns out later that it can be sent, I'll accept your note—or cash, if you have it."

Don had an unpleasant feeling that he was being given a polite brush-off. "Just a moment, sir. I understood that today was the earliest that communication could be expected. Won't conditions be better tomorrow—and still better the next day?"

"Yes, theoretically. But conditions were satisfactory today. There is no communication with Mars."

"But tomorrow?"

"I haven't made myself clear. We tried to signal Mars; we got no answer. So we used the radar check. The bounce came back right on schedule—two thousand two hundred and thirty-eight seconds, no chance of a ghost blip. So we know that the channel was satisfactory and that our signal was getting through. But Schiaparelli Station fails to answer —no communication."

"Out of order, maybe?"

"Most unlikely. It's a dual station. They depend on it for astrogation, you know. No, I'm afraid the answer is obvious."

"Yes?"

"The Federation forces have taken the station over for their own uses. We won't be able to communicate with Mars until they let us."

Don left the manager's office looking as glum as he felt. He ran into Isobel just coming into the building. "Don!"

"Oh—hi, Grandma."

She was excited and failed to notice his mood. "Don—I'm just back from Governor's Island. You know what? They're going to form a women's corps!"

"They are?"

"The bill is in committee now. I can't wait—I'll be in it, of course. I've already put my name in."

"You will be? Yes, I guess you would be." He thought about it and added, "I tried to join up this morning."

She threw her arms around his neck, much to the interest of customers in the lobby. "Don!" She untangled herself, to his blushing relief, and added, "Nobody really expected that of you, Don. After all, it's not your fight; your home is on Mars."

"Well, I don't know. Mars isn't exactly my home, either. And they didn't take me—they told me to wait for my draft call."

"Well—anyway, I'm proud of you."

He went back to the restaurant, feeling ashamed that he had not had the courage to tell her why he had tried to enlist and why he had been turned down. By the time he reached Charlie's place he had about decided to go again to the recruiting office the next day and let them swear him in as a duckfoot. He told himself that the severance of communication with Mars had cut off his last connection with his old life; he might as well accept this new life with both arms. It was better to volunteer than to be dragged.

On second thought he decided to go over to Governor's Island first and send some sort of message to "Sir Isaac"—no use staying in the Ground Forces if his friend could wangle a transfer to the High Guard. It was a dead cinch now that the High Guard would eventually send an expedition to Mars; he might as well be in it. He'd get to Mars yet!

On third thought he decided that it might be well to wait a day or two to hear from "Sir Isaac"; it would certainly be easier to get assigned to the Guard in the first place than to get a transfer later.

Yes, that was the sensible thing to do. Unfortunately it did not make him feel pleased with himself.

That night the Federation attacked.

The attack should not have happened, of course. The rice farmer sergeant had been perfectly right; the Federation could not afford to risk its own great cities to punish the villagers of Venus. He was right—from his viewpoint.

A rice farmer has one logic; men who live by and for power have another and entirely different logic. Their lives are built on tenuous assumptions, fragile as reputation; they cannot afford to ignore a challenge to their power—the Federation could not afford *not* to punish the insolent colonists.

The *Valkyrie,* orbiting Venus in free fall, flashed into radioactive gas without warning. The *Adonis,* in the same orbit a thousand miles astern, saw the explosion and reported it to PHQ at New London; then she, too, became an expanding ball of fire.

Don was awakened from work-drugged sleep by the ululation of sirens. He sat up in the dark, shook his head to clear it, and realized with leaping excitement what the sound was and what it meant. Then he told himself not to be silly; there had been talk lately of holding a night alert—that's what it was: practice.

But he got up and fumbled for the light switch, only to find that the power seemed to be off. He felt around for his clothes, got his right leg in his left trouser leg, tripped. Despite this he was practically dressed by the time a small flickering light came toward him. It was Charlie, carrying a candle in one hand and in the other his favorite cleaver, the one used both for business and social purposes.

The cyclic moan of the sirens continued. "What is it, Charlie?" asked Don. "Do you suppose we've actually been attacked?"

"More likely some dumbhead leaned against the switch."

"Could be. Tell you what—I'm going uptown and find out what's happening."

"Better you stay home."

"I won't be gone long."

In leaving he had to push his way through a crowd of move-overs, all bleating with fright and trying to crowd inside to be close to their friend Charlie. He got through and groped his way to the street, closely escorted by two move-overs who seemed to want to climb into his pockets.

The nights of Venus make the darkest night on Earth feel like twilight. The power seemed to be off all over town; until he turned into Buchanan Street Don could not have counted his own fingers without feeling them. Along Buchanan Street there was an occasional flicker of a lighter and a window or two with dim lights inside. Far up the street someone held a hand torch; Don set his sights on that.

The streets were crowded. He kept bumping into persons in the dark and hearing snatches of speech. "—completely destroyed." "It's a routine drill. I'm a space warden; I *know*." "Why turn off the lights? Their detectors can pick up the power pile in any case." "Hey—get off my feet!" Somewhere along the way he lost his escort; no doubt the gregarians found someone warmer to snuggle up to.

He stopped where the crowd was thickest, around the office of the New London *TIMES*. There were emergency lights inside by which it was possible to read the bulletins being pasted up in the window. At the top was: FLASH BULLETIN (UNOFFICIAL) CRUISER VALKYRIE REPORTED BY CRUISER ADONIS TO HAVE EXPLODED 0030 TONITE. CAUSE NOT REPORTED. LOCAL AUTHORITIES DISCOUNT ATTACK POSSIBILITY, FAVOR POSSIBLE SABOTAGE. FURTHER REPORT EXPECTED COMMANDING OFFICER ADONIS.

BERMUDA (INTERCEPTED) DISORDERS IN WEST
AFRICA TERMED "MINOR INCIDENT" STIRRED UP
BY RELIGIOUS AGITATORS. LOCAL POLICE AS-
SISTED BY FEDERATION PATROL HAVE SITUATION
WELL IN HAND (IT IS CLAIMED).

BERMUDA (INTERCEPTED) A SOURCE CLOSE TO
THE MINISTER OF EXTERNAL AFFAIRS STATES
THAT AN EARLY SETTLEMENT OF THE VENUS IN-
CIDENT IS EXPECTED. REPRESENTATIVES OF IN-
SURGENT COLONISTS SAID TO BE CONFERRING
WITH FEDERATION PLENIPOTENTIARIES SOME-
WHERE ON LUNA IN AN ATMOSPHERE OF GOOD
WILL AND MUTUAL UNDERSTANDING. (NOTE:
THIS REPORT HAS BEEN UNOFFICIALLY DENIED
FROM GOVERNOR'S ISLAND.)

NEW LONDON (PHQ—OFFICIAL) CHIEF OF STAFF
CONFIRMED DAMAGE TO VALKYRIE BUT STATES
EXTENT GREATLY EXAGGERATED. LIST OF CASU-
ALTIES WITHHELD PENDING NOTIFICATION OF
NEXT OF KIN. FULL REPORT FROM COMMANDING
OFFICER ADONIS EXPECTED MOMENTARILY.

FLASH BULLETIN (UNOFFICIAL) CUICUI—UNI-
DENTIFIED SHIPS REPORTED RADAR-TRACKED TO
LANDINGS NORTH AND NORTHWEST OF SETTLE-
MENT. LOCAL GARRISON ALTERED. PHQ REFUSES
COMMENT. NO THIRTY, MORE COMING.

Don crowded up, managed to read the bulletins and
listened to the talk. A faceless voice said, "They wouldn't
and—that's as obsolete as a bayonet charge. If they actually
have blitzed our ships—which I doubt—they would simply
hang in orbit and radio an ultimatum."

"But suppose they did?" someone objected.

"They won't. That bulletin—nerve warfare, that's all. There
are traitors among us."

"That's no news."

A shadowy shape inside was posting a new bulletin. Don
used his elbows and forced his way closer. FLASH—it read
—PHQ (OFFICIAL) PUBLIC INFORMATION OFFI-
CER GENERAL STAFF CONFIRMS REPORT THAT AN
ATTACK HAS BEEN MADE ON SOME OF OUR SHIPS

BY UNIDENTIFIED BUT PRESUMABLY FEDERATION FORCES. THE SITUATION IS FLUID BUT NOT CRITICAL. ALL CITIZENS ARE URGED TO REMAIN IN THEIR HOMES, AVOID PANIC AND LOOSE TALK, AND GIVE FULL CO-OPERATION TO LOCAL AUTHORITIES. MORE DETAILS MAY BE EXPECTED LATER IN THE DAY. REPEAT—STAY HOME AND CO-OPERATE.

A self-appointed crier up front read the bulletin in a loud voice. The crowd took it in silence. While he was reading the sirens died away and the street lights came on. The same voice which had complained of the blackout before now expostulated, "What do they want to turn on the lights for? That's simply inviting them to bomb us!"

No more bulletins showed up; Don backed out, intending to go to the I. T. & T. Building, not with the expectation of finding Isobel there at that hour but in hopes of picking up more news. He had not quite reached the building when he ran into a squad of M. P.'s, clearing the streets. They turned him back and dispersed the crowd at the newspaper office. As Don left the only person there was a dragon with his eyestalks pointed in several directions; he appeared to be reading all the bulletins at once. Don wanted to stop and ask him if he knew "Sir Isaac" and, if so, where his friend might be found, but an M. P. hustled him along. The squad made no attempt to send the dragon about his business; he was left in undisputed possession of the street.

Old Charlie was still up, seated at a table and smoking. His cleaver lay in front of him. Don told him what he had found out. "Charlie, do you think they will land?"

Charlie got up, went to a drawer and got out a whetstone, came back and commenced gently stroking the blade of his cleaver. "Can happen."

"What do you think we ought to do?"

"Go to bed."

"I'm not sleepy. What are you sharpening that thing for?"

"This is my restaurant." He held up the tool, balanced it. "And this is my country." He threw the blade; it turned over twice and *chunked!* into a wood post across the room.

"Be careful with that! You might hurt somebody."

"You go to bed."

"But——"

"Get some sleep. Tomorrow you wish you had." He turned away and Don could get no more out of him. He gave up and went to his own cubbyhole, not intending to sleep but simply to think things over. For a long time after he lay down he could hear the soft swishing of stone on steel.

The sirens awoke him again; it was already light. He went out into the front room; Charlie was still there, standing over the range. "What's going on?"

"Breakfast." With one hand Charlie scooped a fried egg out of a pan, placed it on a slice of bread, while with the other hand he broke another egg into the grease. He slapped a second slice of bread over the egg and handed the sandwich to Don.

Don accepted it and took a large bite before replying, "Thanks. But what are they running the sirens for?"

"Fighting. Listen."

From somewhere in the distance came the muted Wha-Hoom! of an explosion; cutting through the end of it and much nearer was the dry sibilance of a needle beam. Mixed with the fog drifting in the window was a sharp smell of wood burning. "Say!" Don exclaimed, his voice high, "they really did it." Automatically, his mind no longer on food, his jaws clamped down on the sandwich.

Charlie grunted. Don went on, "We ought to get out of here."

"And go where?"

Don had no answer for that. He finished the sandwich while still watching out the window. The smell of smoke grew stronger. A half squad of men showed up at the end of the alley, moving at a dog trot. "Look! Those aren't *our* uniforms!"

"Of course not."

The group paused at the foot of the street, then three men detached themselves and came down the alley, stopping at each door to pound on it. "Outside! Wake up in there—outside, everybody!" Two of them reached the Two Worlds Dining Room; one of them kicked on the door. It came open. "Outside! We're going to set fire to the place."

The man who had spoken was wearing a mottled green uniform with two chevrons; in his hands was a Reynolds one-man gun and on his back the power pack that served it. He looked around. "Say, this is a break!" He turned to the other. "Joe, keep an eye out for the lieutenant." He looked back at Old Charlie. "You, Jack—scramble up about a dozen eggs. Make it snappy—we got to burn this place right away."

Don was caught flat-footed, could think of nothing to do or say. A Reynolds gun brooks no argument. Charlie appeared to feel the same way for he turned back to the range as if to comply.

Then he turned again toward the soldier and in his hand was his cleaver. Don could hardly follow what happened—a flash of blue steel through the air, a meaty, butcher-shop sound, and the cleaver was buried almost to its handle in the soldier's breastbone.

He uttered no cry; he simply looked mildly surprised, then squatted slowly where he stood, his hands still clasping the gun. When he reached the floor, his head bowed forward and the gun slipped from his grasp.

While this went on the other soldier stood still, his own gun at the ready. When his petty officer dropped his gun it seemed to act as a signal to him; he raised his own gun and shot Charlie full in the face. He swung and trained his gun on Don. Don found himself staring into the dark cavity of the projector.

XI

"You Could Go Back to Earth—"

THEY stayed that way for three heart beats . . . then the soldier lowered his weapon about an inch and rapped out, "Outside! Fast!"

Don looked at the gun; the soldier gestured with it.

Don went outside. His heart was raging; he wanted to kill his soldier who had killed Old Charlie. It meant nothing to him that his boss had been killed strictly in accordance with the usages of warfare; Don was in no frame of mind to juggle legalisms. But he was naked against an overpowering weapon; he obeyed. Even as he left the soldier was fanning out with the Reynolds gun; Don heard the hiss as the beam struck dry wood.

The soldier put the torch to the building wastefully; it seemed almost to explode. It was burning in a dozen places as soon as Don was out the door. The soldier jumped out behind him and prodded him in the seat with the hot projector. "Get moving! Up the street." Don broke into a trot, ran out the alley and into Buchanan Street.

The street was filled with people, and green-suited soldiers were herding them uptown. Buildings were burning on both sides of the street; the invaders were destroying the whole city but giving the inhabitants some chance to escape the holocaust. As a part of a faceless mob Don found himself being pushed along and then forced into a side street which was not yet burning. Presently they were beyond the town but the road continued; Don had never been out in this direction but he learned from the talk around him where they were headed—out East Spit.

And into the fenced camp which the new government had used for enemy aliens. Most of the crowd seemed too stunned to care. Somewhere near Don a woman was screaming, her voice rising and falling like a siren.

The camp was crowded to more than ten times its capacity. The camp buildings did not provide standing room; even outdoors the colonists were elbow to elbow. The guards simply shoved them inside and ignored them; they stood there or milled around, while the soft gray ashes of their former homes drifted down on them from the misty sky.

Don had regained his grip on himself during the march out to the camp. Once inside, he tried to find Isobel Costello. He threaded his way through the crowd, searching, asking, peering at faces. More than once he thought he had found her, only to be disappointed—nor did he find her father. Several times he talked to persons who thought they had seen her; each time the clue failed to lead him to her. He began to have waking nightmares of his impetuous young friend dead in the fire, or lying in an alley with a hole in her head.

He was stopped in his weary search by an iron voice bellowing out of the air and reaching all parts of the camp through the camp's announcing system. "Attention!" it called out. "*Quiet!* Attention to orders—this is Colonel Vanistart of the Federation Peace Forces, speaking for the Military Governor of Venus. Conditional amnesty has been granted to all colonists with the exception of those holding office in the rebel government and commissioned officers in the rebel forces. You will be released as quickly as you can be identified. The code of laws in force before the rebellion is restored, subject to such new laws as may be promulgated by the military governor. Attention to Emergency Law Number One! The cities of New London, Buchanan, and CuiCui Town are abolished. Hereafter no community of more than one thousand population will be permitted. Not more than ten persons may assemble without license from the local provost. No military organization may be formed, nor may any colonist possess power weapons under penalty of death."

The voice paused. Don heard someone behind him say, "But what do they expect us to do? We've no place to go, no way to live——"

The rhetorical question was answered at once. The voice went on, "No assistance will be furnished to dispersed rebels by the Federation. Relief to refugees must be provided by colonists who have not been dispossessed. When you are liberated you are advised to spread out into the surrounding countryside and seek temporary shelter with farmers and in the smaller villages."

A bitter voice said, "There's your answer, Clara—they don't give a hoot whether we live or die."

The first voice answered, "But how can we get away? We don't even own a gondola."

"Swim, I guess. Or walk on water."

Soldiers came inside and delivered them to the gate in groups of fifty, cutting them out like cowpunchers handling cattle. Don had pushed toward the gate, hoping to spot Isobel during the processing, and got picked up against his will in the second group. He produced his I. D.s when demanded and immediately ran into a hitch; his name did not appear in the city lists. He explained that he had come in on the last trip of the *Nautilus*.

"Why didn't you say so?" grumbled the soldier doing the checking. He turned and produced another list: "Hannegan . . . Hardecker . . . here it is. Harvey, Donald J.—Yikes! Wait a minute—it's flagged. Hey, sarge! This bird has a polit flag against his name."

"Inside with him," came the bored answer.

Don found himself shoved into the guardroom at the gate, along with a dozen other worried-looking citizens. Almost at once he was conducted on into a little office at the rear. A man who would have seemed tall had he not been so fat stood up and said, "Donald James Harvey?"

"That's right."

The man came to him and looked him over, his face wreathed in a happy grin. "Welcome, my boy, welcome! Am I glad to see you!"

Don looked puzzled. The man went on, "I suppose I should introduce myself—Stanley Bankfield, at your service. Political Officer First Class, I.B.I., at the moment special adviser to his excellency, the Governor."

At the mention of the I.B.I., Don stiffened. The man noticed it—his little, fat-enfolded eyes seemed to notice everything. He said, "Easy, son! I mean you no harm; I'm simply delighted to see you. But I must say you have led me a merry chase—half around the system. At one point I thought you had been killed in the late, lamented *Glory Road,* and I cried tears over your demise. Yes, sir! real tears. But that's over with, and all's well that ends well. So let's have it."

"Have what?"

"Come, now! I know all about you—almost every word you've uttered back to your babyhood. I've even fed sugar to your stock pony, Lazy. So hand it over."

"Hand what over?"

"The ring, the ring!" Bankfield put out a pudgy hand.

"I don't know what you are talking about."

121

Bankfield shrugged mightily. "I am talking about a plastic ring, marked with an initial 'H', given to you by the late Dr. Jefferson. You see, I know what I am talking about; I know you have it—and I mean to have it. An officer in my own service was so stupid as to let you walk out with it—and was broken for it. You wouldn't want that to happen to me, I'm sure. So give it to me."

"Now I know what ring you are talking about," Don answered, "but I don't have it."

"Eh? What's that you are saying? Where is it, then?"

Don's mind was racing ahead. It took him no time at all to decide not to set the I.B.I. to looking for Isobel—no, not if he had to bite his tongue out. "I suppose it's burned up," he answered.

Bankfield cocked his head on one side. "Donald, my boy, I believe you are fibbing to me—I do indeed! You hesitated just a teeny-weeny bit before you answered. No one but a suspicious old man like myself would have noticed it."

"It's true," Don insisted. "Or, at least, I think it is. One of those monkeys you have working for you set fire to the building just as I left. I suppose the building burnt down and the ring with it. But maybe it didn't."

Bankfield looked doubtful. "What building?"

"Two Worlds Dining Room, at the end of Paradise Alley off the foot of Buchanan Street."

Bankfield moved rapidly to the door, gave orders. "Use as many men as needed," he concluded, "and sift every ounce of ash. Move!" He turned back, sighing. "Mustn't neglect any possibilities," he said, "but now we will go back to the probability that you lied. Why should you have taken off your ring in a restaurant?"

"To wash dishes."

"Eh?"

"I was working for my meals, living there. I didn't like putting it in the hot water so I kept it in my room."

Bankfield pursed his lips. "You almost convince me. Your story holds together. And yet, let us both pray that you are deceiving me. If you are and can lead me to the ring, I would be very grateful. You could go back to Earth

122

in style and comfort. I think I could even promise a moderate annuity; we have special funds for such purposes."

"I'm not likely to collect it—unless they find the ring in the restaurant."

"Dear me! In that case I don't suppose either one of us will go back to Earth. No, sir, I think that in such a case I would find it better to stay right here—devoting my declining years to making your life miserable."

He smiled. "I was joking—I'm sure we'll find the ring, with your help. Now, Don, tell me what you did with it." He put an arm around Don's shoulders in a fatherly fashion.

Don tried to shrug the arm off, found that he could not. Bankfield went on, "We could settle it quickly if I had proper equipment at hand. Or I could do this—" The arm around Don's shoulders dropped suddenly; Bankfield seized Don's left little finger and bent it back sharply. Involuntarily Don grunted with pain.

"Sorry! I don't like such methods. The operator, in an excess of zeal, frequently damages the client so that no truth of any sort is forthcoming. No, Don, I think we will wait a few minutes while I get word to the medical department—sodium pentothal seems to be indicated. It will make you more co-operative, don't you think?" Bankfield stepped again to the door. "Orderly! Put this one on ice. And send in that Mathewson character."

Don was conducted outside the guardhouse and into a pen, a fenced enclosure used to receive prisoners. It was some thirty feet wide and a hundred feet long; one of its longer sides was common with the fence that ran around the entire camp, the other shut it off from the free world. The only entrance to it lay through the guardhouse.

There were several dozen prisoners in the receiving pen, most of them civilian men, although Don saw a number of women and quite a few officers of the Middle Guard and of the Ground Forces—still in uniform but disarmed.

He at once checked the faces of the women; none was Isobel. He had not expected to find her, yet found himself vastly disappointed. His time was running out; he realized with panic that it was probably only minutes until he would be held down, drug injected into his veins—and be turned thereby into a babbling child with no will to resist their questioning. He had never been subjected to narco-interrogation but he knew quite well what the drug would do. Even deep-hypnotic suggestion could not protect against it in the hands of a skilled operator.

Somehow he felt sure that Bankfield was skilled.

He went to the far end of the pen, pointlessly, as a frightened animal will retreat to the back of a cage. He stood there, staring up at the top of the fence several feet above his head. The fence was tight and strong, proof against almost anything but a dragon, but one could get handholds in the mesh—it could be climbed. However, above the mesh were three single strands of wire; every ten feet or so on the lowest strand was a little red sign—a skull-and-crossbones and the words HIGH VOLTAGE.

Don glanced back over his shoulder. The everpresent fog, reinforced by smoke from the burning city, almost obscured the guardhouse. The breeze had shifted and the smoke was getting thicker; he felt reasonably sure that no one could see him but other prisoners.

He tried it, found that his shoes would not go into the mesh, kicked them off and tried again.

"Don't!" said a voice behind him.

Don looked back. A major of the Ground Forces, cap missing and one sleeve torn and bloody, stood behind him. "Don't try it," the major said reasonably. "It will kill you quickly. I know; I supervised its installation."

Don dropped to the ground. "Isn't there some way to switch it off?"

"Certainly—outside." The officer grinned wryly. "I took care of that. A locked switch in the guardhouse—and another at the main distribution board in the city. Nowhere else." He coughed. "Pardon me—the smoke."

Don looked toward the burning city. "The distribution board back in the powerhouse," he said softly. "I wonder——"

"Eh?" The major followed his glance. "I don't know—I couldn't say. The powerhouse is fireproof."

A voice behind them in the mist shouted, "Harvey! Donald J. Harvey! Front and center!"

Don swarmed up the fence.

He hesitated just before touching the lowest of the three strands, flipped it with the back of his hand. Nothing happened—then he was over and falling. He lit badly, hurting a wrist, but scrambled to his feet and ran.

There were shouts behind him; without stopping he risked a look over his shoulder. Someone else was at the top of the fence. Even as he looked he heard the hiss of a beam. The figure jerked and contracted, like a fly touched by flame.

The figure raised its head. Don heard the major's voice in a clear triumphant baritone: *"Venus and Freedom!"* He fell back inside the fence.

XII

Wet Desert

Don plunged ahead, not knowing where he was going, not caring as long as it was away. Again he heard the angry, deadly hissing; he cut to the left and ran faster, then cut back again beyond a clump of witch's brooms. He pounded ahead, giving it all he had, with his breath like dry steam in his throat—then skidded to a stop at water's edge.

He stood still for a moment, looked and listened. Nothing to see but grey mist, nothing to hear but the throbbing of his own heart. No, not quite nothing—someone shouted in the distance and he heard the sounds of booted feet crashing through the brush. It seemed to come from the right; he turned left and trotted along the waterfront, his eyes open for a gondola, a skiff, anything that would float.

The bank curled back to the left; he followed it, then stopped as he realized that it was leading him to the narrow neck of land that joined Main Island to East Spit. It was a cinch, he thought, that there would be a guard at the bottleneck; it seemed to him that there had been one there when he and the other dispossessed had been herded across it to the prison camp.

He listened—yes, they were still behind him—and flanking him. There was nothing in front of him but the bank curving back to certain capture.

For a moment his face was contorted in an agony of frustration, then his features suddenly relaxed to serenity and he stepped firmly into the water and walked away from the land.

Don could swim, in which respect he differed from most Venus colonials. On Venus no one ever swims; there is no water fit to swim in. Venus has no moon to pile up tides; the solar tide disturbs her waters but little. The waters never freeze, never approach the critical 4° C. which causes terrestrial lakes and streams and ponds to turn over and "ventilate." The planet is almost free of weather in the boisterous sense. Her waters lie placid on their surface—and accumulate vileness underneath, by the year, by the generation, by the eon.

Don walked straight out, trying not to think of the black and sulphurous muck he was treading in. The water was shallow; fifty yards out with the shoreline dim behind him, he was still in only up to his knees. He glanced back and decided to go out farther; if he could not see the shore, then they could not see him. He reminded himself that he would have to keep his wits about him not to get turned around.

Presently the bottom suddenly dropped away a foot or more; he stepped off the edge; lost his balance and thrashed around; recovered himself and scrambled back up on the ledge, congratulating himself that he had not gotten his face and eyes into the stuff.

He heard a shout and almost at once the sound of water striking a hot stove, enormously amplified. Ten feet away from him a cloud of steam lifted from the water's surface, climbed lazily into the mist. He cringed and wanted to dodge, but there was no way to dodge. The shouting resumed and the sounds carried clearly across the water, muffled by the fog but still plain: "Over here! Over here! He's taken to the water."

Much more distantly he heard the answer: "Coming!"

Most cautiously Don moved forward, felt the edge of the

drop off, tried it and found that he could still stand beyond it, almost up to his armpits but still wading. He was moving forward slowly, trying to avoid noise and minding his precarious, half-floating balance, when he heard the sibilant sound of the beam.

The soldier back on the bank had imagination; instead of firing again at random into the drifting mist he was fanning the flat surface of the water, doing his best to keep his beam horizontal and playing it like a hose. Don squatted down until his face alone was out of the water.

The beam passed only inches over his head; he could hear it pass, smell the ozone.

The hissing stopped abruptly to be followed by the age-old, monotonous cursing of the barrackroom. "But, sergeant—" someone protested.

"I'll 'sergeant' you! Alive—do you hear? You heard the orders. If you've killed him, I'll take you apart with a rusty knife. No, I won't; I'll turn you over to Mr. Bankfield. You hopeless fool!"

"But, sergeant, he was escaping by water; I had to stop him."

" 'But sergeant!' 'But sergeant!'—is that all you can say! Get a boat! Get a snooper! Get a two-station portable bounce rig. Call base and find out if they've got a copter down."

"Where would I get a boat?"

"Get one! He can't get away. We'll find him—or his body. If it's his body, you'd better cut your throat."

Don listened, then moved silently forward—or away from the direction the voices seemed to come from. He could no longer tell true direction; there was nothing but the black surface of water and a horizon of mist. For some distance the bottom continued fairly level, then he realized that it was again dropping away. He was forced to stop, able to wade no further.

He thought it over, trying to avoid panic. He was still close to Main Island with nothing but mist between himself and the shore. It was a certainty that with proper search gear—infra-red or any of the appropriate offspring of radar—they could pin him like a beetle to cork. It was merely a matter of waiting for the gear to be brought up.

Should he surrender now and get out of this poisonous swill? Surrender and go back and tell Bankfield to find Isobel Costello if he wanted the ring? He let himself sink forward and struck out strongly, swimming breast stroke to try to keep his face out of the water.

Breast stroke was far from being his strongest stroke and it was made worse by trying so hard to keep his face dry. His neck began to ache; presently the ache spread through his shoulder muscles and into his back. Indefinite time and endless gallons later he ached everywhere, even to his eyeballs—yet for all he could tell about it he might have been swimming in a bathtub, one whose walls were grey mist. It did not seem possible that, in the archipelago which made up Buchanan Province, one could swim so far without running into *something* . . . a sand spit, a mud bar.

He stopped to tread water, barely moving his tired legs and fluttering his palms. He thought he heard the rushing sound of a powered boat, but he could not be sure. At that moment he would not have cared; capture would have been relief. But the sound, or ghost of a sound, died away and he was again in a grey and featureless wilderness.

He arched his back to shift again to swimming and his toe struck bottom. Gingerly he felt for it—yes, bottom . . . with his chin out of water. He stood for a moment or two and rested, then felt around. Bottom dropped away on one side, seemed level or even to rise a little in another direction.

Shortly his shoulders were out with his feet still in the muck. Feeling his way like a blind man, his eyes useless save for balancing, he groped out the contour, finding bits that rose, then forced to retreat as the vein played out.

He was out of water to his waist when his eyes spotted a darker streak through the fog; he went toward it, was again up to his neck. Then the bottom rose rapidly; a few moments later he scrambled up on dry land.

He did not have the courage yet to do anything more than move inland a few feet and place between himself and the water a clump of *Chika* trees. Screened thus from search operations conducted from boats he looked himself over. Clinging to his legs were a dozen or more mud lice, each as large as a child's hand. With repugnance he brushed them off, then removed his shorts and shirt, found several more and disposed of them. He told himself that he was lucky not to have encountered anything worse—the dragons had many evolutionary cousins, bearing much the same relationship to them that gorillas do to men. Many of these creatures are amphibious—another reason why Venus colonials do not swim.

Reluctantly Don put his wet and filthy clothes back on, sat down with his back to a tree trunk, and rested. He was still doing so when he again heard the sound of a power boat; this time there was no mistaking it. He sat still, depending on the trees to cover him and hoping that it would go away.

It came in close to shore and cruised along it to his right. He was beginning to feel relief when the turbine stopped. In the stillness he could hear voices. "We'll have to reconnoiter this hunk of mud. Okay, Curly—you and Joe."

"What does this guy look like, corporal?"

"Now, I'll tell you—the captain didn't say. He's a young fellow, though, about your age. You just arrest anything that walks. He's not armed."

"I wish I was back in Birmingham."

"Get going."

Don got going, too—in the other direction, as fast and as silently as possible. The island was fairly well covered; he hoped that it was large as well—a precarious game of hide-and-seek was all the tactics he could think of. He had covered perhaps a hundred yards when he was scared out of his wits by movement up ahead; he realized with desperation that the boat party might have landed two patrols.

His panic died down when he discovered that what he was seeing were not men but gregarians. They spotted him, too, and came dancing up, bleating welcome, and crowding up against him.

"Quiet!" he said in a sharp whisper. "You'll get me caught!"

The move-overs paid no attention to that; they wanted

to play. He endeavored to pay no attention to them but moved forward again, closely accompanied by the whole group, some five. He was still wondering how to keep from being loved to death—or at least back into captivity—when they came out into the clearing.

Here was the rest of the herd, more than two hundred head, from babies that butted against his knees up to the grey-bearded old patriarch, fat in the belly and reaching as high as Don's shoulder. They all welcomed him and wanted him to stay a while.

One thing that had worried him was now cleared up—he had not swum in a circle and blundered back onto Main Island. The only move-overs on Main Island were half-domesticated scavengers such as those which had hung around the restaurant; there were no herds.

It suddenly occurred to him that it was barely possible that he might turn the ubiquitous friendliness of the bipeds into an advantage rather than a sure give-away. They would not let him be; that was sure. If he left the herd, some of them were certain to trail along, bleating and snorting and making themselves and him conspicuous. On the other hand—

He moved straight out into the clearing, pushing his friends aside as he went. He shoved himself right into the center of the herd and sat down on the ground.

Three of the babies promptly climbed into his lap. He let them stay. Adults and half-grown bucks crowded around him, bleating and snuffling and trying to nuzzle the top of his head. He let them—he was now surrounded by a wall of flesh. From time to time one of the inner circle would be shouldered out of the way and would go back to grazing but there were always enough around him to block out his view of his surroundings. He waited.

After a considerable time he heard more excited bleating from the fringe of the herd. For a moment he thought his personal guard would be seduced away by this new excitement, but the inner circle preferred to keep their privileged positions; the wall held. Again he heard voices.

"For Pete's sake—it's a whole flock of those silly billies!" Then—"Hey! Get down! Quit licking my face!"

Curly's voice replied, "I think he's fallen in love with you, Joe. Say—Soapy said to arrest anything that walks: shall we take this one back to him?"

"Stow it!" There were sounds of scuffling, then the high bleating of a move-over both surprised and hurt.

"Maybe we ought to burn one and take it back anyway," Curly went on. "I hear they are mighty tasty eating."

"You turn this into a hunting party and Soapy will haul you up before the Old Man. Come on—we got work to do."

Don could follow their progress around the edge of the herd. He could even tell by the sounds when the two soldiers managed to cuff and kick the most persistent of the creatures off their trail. He continued to sit there long after they were gone, tickling the chin of a baby which had gone to sleep in his lap, and resting himself.

Presently it began to grow dark. The herd started to bed down for the night. By the time it was fully dark they were all lying down except the sentries around the edge. Because he was dead tired and completely lacking in any plan of action Don bedded down with them, his head cradled on a soft and velvety back and himself in turn half supporting a couple of youngsters.

For a while he thought about his predicament, then he thought about food and, even more urgently, water. Then he thought about nothing.

The herd stirred and he awakened. There was much snorting and stomping mixed with the whimpering complaints of the young, still not fully awake. Don got his bearings and got to his own feet; he knew vaguely what to expect—the herd was about to migrate. Gregarians rarely grazed the same island two days in a row. They slept the first part of the night, then moved out before dawn when their natural enemies were least active. They forded from one island to another, using paths through the water known —possibly by instinct—to the herd leaders. For that matter, gregarians could swim, but they rarely did so.

Don thought: well, I'll soon be rid of them. Nice people— but too much is too much. Then he thought better of it—if the move-overs were moving to another island it was sure that it would not be Main Island and it would certainly have to be farther away from Main Island than was this one. What could he lose?

He felt a bit light-headed but the logic seemed right; when the herd moved out he worked his way up near the van. The leader took them down the island about a quarter of a mile, then stepped off into the water. It was still so nearly pitch dark that Don was not aware of it until he too stepped into it. It was only up to his ankles and did not get much deeper. Don splashed along almost at a dogtrot, trying to stay inside the body of the herd so that he would run no chances of blundering into deeper water in the darkness. He hoped that this was not one of the migrations involving swimming.

It began to grow truly light and the pace quickened; Don was hard put to keep up. At one point the old buck in the lead stopped, snorted, and made a sharp turn; Don could not guess why he had turned, for the morning mist was very thick and one piece of water looked exactly like another. Yet the way chosen turned out to be shallow. They followed it for another kilometer or more, twisting and turning at times, then at last the leader clambered up a bank with Don on his heels.

Don threw himself down, exhausted. The old buck stopped, plainly puzzled, while the herd gained the land and crowded around them. The leader snorted and looked disgusted, then turned away and continued his duty of leading his people to good pasture. Don pulled himself together and followed them.

They were just coming out of the trees that hedged the shore when Don saw a fence off to the right. He felt like singing. "So long, folks!" he called out. "Here's where I get off." He headed for the fence, while the main herd moved on. When he reached the fence he reluctantly slapped and swatted his attendants until he managed to shoo them off, then headed along the wire. Eventually, he told himself, I will find a gate and that will lead me to people. It did not matter much who the people were; they would feed him and let him rest and help him to hide from the invaders.

The fog was very thick; it was good to have the fence

to guide him. He stumbled along by it, feeling feverish and somewhat confused, but cheerful.

"Halt."

Don froze automatically, shook his head and tried to remember where he was. "I've got you spotted," the voice went on. "Move forward slowly with your hands up."

Don strained his eyes to see through the fog, wondered if he dared to run for it. But, with a feeling of utter and final defeat, he realized that he had run as far as he could.

XIII

Fog-Eaters

"SNAP out of it!" the voice said, "or I shoot."

"Okay," he answered dully and moved forward with his hands over his head. A few paces advance let him see a man's shape; a few more and he made out a soldier with a hand gun trained on him. His eyes were covered by snooper goggles, making him look like some bug-eyed improbability from another planet.

The soldier halted Don again a few steps from him, made him turn around slowly. When Don turned back he had shoved the snoopers up on his forehead, revealing pleasant blue eyes. He lowered his gun. "Jack, you're sure a mess," he commented. "What in the name of the Egg have you been doing?"

It was only then that Don realized that the soldier was wearing not the mottled green of the Federation but the tans of the Ground Forces of Venus Republic.

The soldier's commanding officer, a Lieutenant Busby, tried to question him in the kitchen of the farm house inside the fence, but he saw very quickly that the prisoner was in no shape to be questioned. He turned Don over to the farmer's wife for food, a hot bath, and emergency medical attention. It was late that afternoon that Don, much refreshed and with the patches left by the mud lice covered with poultices, finally gave an account of himself.

Busby listened him out and nodded. "I'll take your word for it, mainly because it is almost inconceivable that a Federation spy could have been where you were, dressed the way you were, and in the shape you were in." He went on to question him closely about what he had seen in New London, how many soldiers there seemed to be, how they were armed, and so forth. Unfortunately Don could not tell him much. He did recite "Emergency Law Number One" as closely as he could remember it.

Busby nodded, "We got it over Mr. Wong's radio." He hooked a thumb at the corner of the room. He thought for a moment. "They played it smart; they took a leaf from Commodore Higgins' book and played it real smart. They didn't bomb our cities; they just bombed our ships—then they moved in and burned us out."

"Have we got any ships left?" Don asked.

"I don't know. I doubt it—but it doesn't matter."

"Huh?"

"Because they played it too smart. There's nothing left they can do to us; from here on they're fighting the fog. And we fog-eaters know this planet better than they do."

Don was allowed to rest up the balance of that day and the following night. By listening to the gossip of the soldiers he came to the conclusion that Busby was not simply an optimist; the situation was not completely hopeless. It was admittedly very bad; so far as anyone knew all the ships of the High Guard had been destroyed. The *Valkyrie*, the *Nautilus*, and the *Adonis* were reported bombed, and with them Commodore Higgins and most of his men. There was no word of the *Spring Tide*—which meant nothing; what little information they had was compounded of equal parts rumor and Federation official propaganda.

The Middle Guard might have saved some of their ships, might have them hidden out in the bush, but the usefulness at this time of superstratospheric shuttles which required unmovable launching catapults was conjectural. As for the Ground Forces a good half of them had been captured or killed at Buchanan Island Base and at lesser garrisons. While the enlisted survivors were being released, the only officers still free were such as Lieutenant Busby, those who had been on detached duty when the attack came. Busby's unit had been manning a radar station outside New London; he had saved his command by abandoning the now-useless station.

The civil government of the baby republic was, of course, gone; almost every official had been captured. The command organization of the armed forces was equally out of action, captured in the initial attack. This raised a point that puzzled Don; Busby did not act as if his commanding generals were missing; he continued to behave as if he were a unit commander of an active military organization, with task and function clearly defined. *Esprit de corps* was high among his men; they seemed to expect months, perhaps years of bush warfare, harrying and raiding the Federation forces, but eventual victory at the end.

As one of them put it to Don, "They can't catch us. We know these swamps; they don't. They won't be able to go ten miles from the city, even with boat radar and dead-reckoning bugs. We'll sneak in at night and cut their throats —and sneak out again for breakfast. We won't let them lift a ton of radioactive off this planet, nor an ounce of drugs. We'll make it so expensive in money and men that they'll get sick of it and go home."

Don nodded. "Sick of fighting the fog, as Lieutenant Busby puts it."

"Busby?"

"Huh? Lieutenant Busby—your C. O."

"Is that his name? I didn't catch it." Don's face showed bewilderment. The soldier went on, "I've only been here since morning, you see. I was turned loose with the other duckfeet from the Base and was dragging my tail back home, feeling lower than swamp muck. I stopped off here, meaning to cadge a meal from Wong, and found the Lieutenant here—Busby, did you say?—with a going concern. He attached me and put me back on duty. I tell you, it put the heart back into me. Got a light on you?"

Before he turned in that night—in Mr. Wong's barn, with two dozen soldiers—Don had found that most of those present were not of Busby's original detail, which had consisted of only five men, all electronics technicians. The rest were stragglers, now formed into a guerilla platoon. As yet few of them had arms; they made up for that in restored morale.

Before he went to sleep Don had made up his mind. He would have looked up Lieutenant Busby at once but decided that it would not do to disturb the officer so late at night. He woke up next morning to find the soldiers gone. He rushed out, found Mrs. Wong feeding her chickens, and was directed by her down to the waterfront. There Busby was superintending the moving out of his command. Don rushed up to him. "Lieutenant! May I have a word with you?"

Busby turned impatiently. "I'm busy."

"Just a single moment—please!"

"Well, speak up."

"Just this—where can I go to enlist?" Busby frowned; Don raced ahead with explanation, insisting that he had been trying to join up when the attack came.

"If you meant to enlist, I should think you would have done so long ago. Anyway, by your own story you've lived a major portion of your life on Earth. You're not one of us."

"Yes, I am!"

"I think you're a kid with your head stuffed with romantic notions. You're not old enough to vote."

"I'm old enough to fight."

"What can you do?"

"Uh, well, I'm a pretty good shot, with a hand gun anyway."

"What else?"

Don thought rapidly; it had not occurred to him that soldiers were expected to have anything more than willingness. Ride horseback? It meant nothing here. "Uh, I talk 'true speech'—fairly well."

"That's useful—we need men who can palaver with the dragons. What else?"

Don thought about the fact that he had been able to make his escape through the bush without disaster—but the Lieutenant knew that; it simply proved that he was truly a fog-eater in spite of his mixed background. He decided that

Busby would not be interested in the details of his ranch school education. "Well, I can wash dishes."

Busby grudged a faint smile. "That is unquestionably a soldierly virtue. Nevertheless, Harvey, I doubt if you're suited. This won't be parade-ground soldiering. We'll live off the country and probably never get paid at all. It means going hungry, going dirty, always on the move. You not only risk being killed in action; if you are captured, you'll be burned for treason."

"Yes, sir. I figured that out last night."

"And you still want to join?"

"Yes, sir."

"Hold up your right hand."

Don did so. Busby continued. "Do you solemnly swear to uphold and defend the Constitution of the Venus Republic against all enemies, domestic and foreign; and to serve faithfully in the armed forces of the Republic for the duration of this emergency unless sooner discharged by competent authority; and to obey the lawful orders of superior officers placed over you?"

Don took a deep breath. "I do."

"Very well, soldier—get in the boat."

"Yes, sir!"

There were many, many times thereafter that Don regretted having enlisted—but so has every man who ever volunteered for military service. More of the time he was reasonably content, though he would have denied this sincerely—he acquired considerable talent at the most common of soldiers' pastimes, griping about the war, the weather, the food, the mud, the stupidities of high command. The old soldier can substitute for recreation, or even for rest or food, this ancient, conventional, and harmless form of literary art.

He learned the ways of the guerilla—to infiltrate without a sound, to strike silently, and to fade back into the dark and the mist before the alarm can be raised. Those who learned it lived; those who did not, died. Don lived. He learned other things—to sleep for ten minutes when opportunity offered, to come fully and quietly awake at a touch

or a sound, to do without sleep for a night, or two nights—
or even three. He acquired deep lines around his mouth, lines
beyond his years, and a white, puckered scar on his left
forearm.

He did not stay long with Busby but was transferred to
a company of gondola infantry operating between CuiCui
and New London. They called themselves proudly "Marsten's Raiders"; he was assigned as "true speech" interpreter
for his outfit. While most colonials can whistle a few phrases
of dragon talk—or, more usually, can understand a bit of
pidgin sufficient for buying and selling—few of them can con-
verse freely in it. Don, for all his lack of practice during
his years on Earth, had been taught it young and taught it
well by a dragon who had taken an interest in him as a
child. And both his parents used it as easily as they did
Basic English; Don had been drilled in it by daily use at
home until he was eleven.

The dragons were of great use to the resistance fighters;
while not belligerents themselves their sympathies lay with
the colonials—more accurately, they despised the Federation soldiers. The colonials had managed to make a home
on Venus through getting along with the dragons—an enlight-
ened-self-interest policy instituted by Cyrus Buchanan himself. To a human born on Venus there was never any doubt
that there existed another race—dragons—as intelligent, as
wealthy, and as civilized as their own. But to the great
majority of the Federation soldiers, new to the planet, the
dragons were merely ugly, uncouth animals, incapable of
speech and giving themselves airs, arrogating to themselves
privileges that no animal had a right to claim.

This orientation cut below the conscious level; no general order issued to the Federation troops, no amount of
disciplinary action for violations, could cope with it. It was
stronger and less reasoned than any analogous Earthly trouble—white versus black, gentile versus Jew, Roman versus
barbarian, or whatever—had ever been. The very officers
issuing the orders could not feel the matter correctly; they
were not Venus born. Even the governor's prime political
adviser, the shrewd and able Stanley Bankfield, could
not really grasp that one does not ingratiate oneself with a

dragon by (so to speak) patting him on the head and talking down.

Two serious incidents had set the pattern on the very day of the original attack; in New London a dragon—the same one Don had seen reading the *Times*' bulletins—had been, not killed, but seriously damaged by a flamethrower; he had been silent partner in the local bank and lessor of many rich thorium pits. Still worse, in CuiCui a dragon had been killed—by a rocket; through mischance he had had his mouth open. And *this* dragon had been related collaterally to the descendants of the Great Egg.

It does not do to antagonize highly intelligent creatures each of whom is physically equivalent to, say three rhinoceri or a medium tank. Nevertheless they were not themselves belligerents, as our convention of warfare is not part of their culture. They work in different ways to their ends.

When in the course of his duties Don had to speak to dragons he sometimes inquired whether or not this particular citizen or the dragon nation knew his friend "Sir Isaac"—using, of course, "Sir Isaac's" true name. He found that those who could not claim personal acquaintance at least knew of him; he found, too, that it raised his own prestige to claim acquaintanceship. But he did not attempt to send a message to "Sir Isaac"; there was no longer any occasion for it—no need to try to wangle a transfer to a High Guard that no longer existed.

He did try and try repeatedly to learn what had happened to Isobel Costello—through refugees, through dragons, and through the increasingly numerous clandestine resistance fighters who could move fairly freely from one side to the other. He never found her. He heard once that she was confined in the prison camp on East Spit; he heard again that she and her father had been deported to Earth—neither rumor could be confirmed. He suspected, with a dull, sick feeling inside, that she had been killed in the original attack.

He was grieved about Isobel herself—not about the ring that he had left with her. He had tried to guess what it could possibly be about the ring which would cause him to be chased from planet to planet. He could not think of an answer and concluded that Bankfield, for all his superior airs, had been mistaken; the important thing must have been the wrapping paper but the I.B.I. had been too stupid to figure it out. Then he quit thinking about it at all; the ring was gone and that was that.

As for his parents and Mars—sure, sure, someday! Someday when the war was over and ships were running again—in the meantime why let the worry mice gnaw at one's mind?

His company was at this time spread out through four islands south-southwest of New London; they had been camped there for three days, about the longest they ever stayed in one place. Don, being attached to headquarters, was on the same island as Captain Marsten and was, at the moment, stretched out in his hammock which he had slung between two trees in the midst of a clump of broom.

The company headquarters runner sought him out and awakened him—by standing well clear and giving the hammock rope a sharp tap. Don came instantly awake, a knife in his hand. "Easy!" cautioned the runner. "The Old Man wants to see you."

Don made a rhetorical and most ungracious suggestion as to what the Captain could do about it and slid silently to his feet. He stopped to roll up the hammock and stuff it into his pocket—it weighed only four ounces and had cost the Federation a nice piece of change on cost-plus contract. Don was very careful of it; its former owner had not been careful and now had no further need for it. He gathered up his weapons as well.

The company commander was sitting at a field desk under a screen of boughs. Don slid into his presence and waited. Marsten looked up and said, "Got a special job for you, Harvey. You move out at once."

"Change in the plan?"

"No, you won't be on tonight's raid. A high mugamug among the dragons wants palaver. You're to go to see him. At once."

Don thought it over. "Cripes, Skipper, I was looking forward to tonight's scramble. I'll go tomorrow—those people don't care about time; they're patient."

"That'll do, soldier. I'm putting you on leave status; according to the despatch from HQ, you may be gone quite a while."

Don looked up sharply. "If I'm ordered to go, it's not leave; it's detached duty."

"You're a mess hall lawyer at heart, Harvey."

"Yes, sir."

"Turn in your weapons and take off your insignia; you'll make the first leg of the trip as a jolly farmer boy. Pick up some props from stores. Larsen will boat you. That's all."

"Yes, sir." Don turned to go, adding, "Good hunting tonight, Skipper."

Marsten smiled for the first time. "Thanks, Don."

The first part of the trip was made through channels so narrow and devious that electronic seeing devices could reach no further than could the bare eye. Don slept through most of it, his head pillowed on a sack of sour-corn seed. He did not worry about the job ahead—no doubt the officer he was to interpret for, whoever he was, would rendezvous and let him know what he was to do.

Early in the next afternoon they reached the brink of the Great South Sea and Don was transferred to a crazy wagon, a designation which applied to both boat and crew—a flat, jet-propelled saucer fifteen feet across manned by two young extroverts who feared neither man nor mud. The upperworks of the boat were covered by a low, polished cone of sheet metal intended to reflect horizontal radar waves upward, or vice versa. It could not protect against that locus in the sky, cone-shaped like the reflector itself, where reflections would bounce straight back to originating stations—but the main dependence was on speed in any case.

Don lay flat on the bottom of the boat, clinging to handholds and reflecting on the superior advantages of rocket flight, while the crazy wagon skipped and slid over the surface of the sea. He tried not to think about what would happen if the speeding boat struck a floating log or one of the larger denizens of the water. They covered nearly three hundred kilometers in somewhat less than two hours, then the boat skidded and slewed to a stop. "End of the line," called out the downy-cheeked skipper. "Have your baggage checks ready. Women and children use the center escalator." The anti-radar lid lifted.

Don stood up on wobbly legs. "Where are we?"

"Dragonville-by-the-Mud. There's your welcoming committee. Mind your step."

Don peered through the mist. There seemed to be several dragons on the shore. He stepped over the side, went into mud to his boot tops, scrambled up to firmer soil. Behind him, the crazy wagon lowered its cover and gunned away at once, going out of sight while still gathering speed. "They might at least have waved," Don muttered and turned back to the dragons. He was feeling considerably perplexed; there seemed to be no men around and he had been given no instructions. He wondered if the officer he had expected to find—surely by this time!—had failed to run the gauntlet safely.

There were seven of the dragons, now moving toward him. He looked them over and whistled a polite greeting, while thinking how much one dragon looks like another. Then the center one of the seven spoke to him in an accent richly reminiscent of fish-and-chips. "Donald, my dear boy! How very happy I am to see you! Shucks!"

XIV

"Let's Have It, Then."

DON gulped and stared and almost lost track of his manners. "Sir Isaac! Sir Isaac!" He stumbled toward him.

It is not practical to shake hands with a dragon, kiss it, nor hug it. Don contented himself with beating Sir Isaac's armored sides with his fists while trying to regain control of himself. Long-suppressed emotions shook him, spoiling voice and vision. Sir Isaac waited patiently, then said, "Now, Donald, if I may present my family——"

Don pulled himself together, cleared his throat, and wet his whistle. None of the others had a voder; it was possible that they did not even understand Basic. *"May they all die beautifully!"*

"We thank you."

A daughter, a son, a granddaughter, a grandson, a great granddaughter, a great grandson—counting Sir Isaac himself, a *four* generation welcome, only one short of maximum dragon protocol; Don was overwhelmed. He knew that Sir Isaac was friendly to him, but he decided that this degree of ceremony must be a compliment to his parents. *"My Father and my Mother thank you all for the kindness you do to their egg."*

"As the first egg, so the last. We are very happy to have you here, Donald."

A dragon visitor, honored by an escort, would have made a leisurely progress to the family seat flanked by the family members. But a dragon's leisurely progress is about twice as fast as a brisk walk for a man. Sir Isaac settled himself down and said, "Suppose you borrow my legs, dear boy; we have considerable distance to go."

"Oh, I can walk!"

"Please—I insist."

"Well——"

" 'Upsy-daisy'! then—if I recall the idiom correctly."

Don climbed aboard and settled himself just abaft the last pair of eyestalks; they turned around and surveyed him. He found that Sir Isaac had thoughtfully had two rings riveted to his neck plates to let him hold on. "All set?"

"Yes, indeed."

The dragon reared himself up again and they set out, with Don feeling like Toomai-of-the-Elephants.

They went up a crowded dragon path so old that it was impossible to tell whether it was an engineering feat or a natural conformation. The path paralleled the shore for a mile or so; they passed dragons at work in their watery fields, then the path swung inland. Shortly, in the dry uplands, his party turned out of the traffic into a tunnel. This was definitely art, not nature; it was one of the sort the floor of which slides quietly and rapidly away in the direction one walks (provided the walker is a dragon or weighs as much as a dragon); their ambling gait was multiplied by

143

a considerable factor. Don could not judge the true speed nor the distance covered.

They came at last out into a great hall, large even for dragons; the flowing floor merged into the floor of the hall imperceptibly and stopped. Here were gathered the rest of the tribe symbolized by the seven who had met him. But Don was not required then to rack his brain for compliments, but was taken, still in accordance with etiquette, at once to his own chambers to rest and refresh himself.

The chambers were merely comfortable by Venerian standards; to Don, of course, they were huge. The wallowing trough in the center of the main room was less than six feet deep only at the ramp and it was long enough for him to take several strokes—which he did very soon with great pleasure. The water was as pure as the Sea he had just crossed was dirty and it was, as nearly as he could tell, heated for him to exactly the 98.6° of a human's blood.

He turned over on his back and floated, staring up into the artificial mist that concealed the remote ceiling. This, he thought, was certainly the life! It was the best bath he had had since—well, since that dilly of a bath in the *Caravansary* back in New Chicago, how long ago? Don thought with a sudden twinge of nostalgia that his class in school had graduated long since.

Growing tired even of such luxury he climbed out, then took his clothes and scrubbed out ancient dirt as best he could, while wishing for detergent, or even for the grey homemade soap the farmers used. He paddled around in bare feet, looking for somewhere to hang his wash. In the "small" retiring room he stopped suddenly.

Supper was ready. Someone had set a table for him, complete to fine napery—a card table, it was, with "Grand Rapids" spelled out in its lines. The chairs drawn up to it actually did have "Grand Rapids" stamped into its under side; Don turned it over and looked.

The table had been set in accordance with human customs. True, the soup was in the coffee cup and the soup plate contained coffee, but Don was in no mood to cavil about such details—they were both hot. So was the sour bread toast and the scrambled eggs—shell eggs, if he was a judge.

He spread his wet clothes on the warm, tiled floor, hastily patted them smooth, drew up the chair and fell to. "As you say, Skipper," he muttered, "we never had it so good."

There was a foam mattress on the floor of another bay of the same room; Don did not need to look to see that it was Greenie general issue (officers). There was no bedframe and no blankets, but neither was necessary. Knowing that he would not be disturbed nor expected to put in an appearance until it suited him, he spread himself out on it after dinner. He was very tired, he now realized, and he certainly had much to think about.

The reappearance of Sir Isaac caused buried memories to lift their heads, fresh and demanding. He thought again of his school, wondered where his roommate was. Had he joined up—on the other side? He hoped not . . . yet knew in his heart that Jack had. You did what you had to do, judging it from where you were. Jack wasn't his enemy, couldn't be. Good old Jack! He hoped strongly that the wild chances of war would never bring them face to face.

He wondered if Lazy still remembered him.

He saw again Old Charlie's face, suddenly blasted out of human shape . . . and again his heart raged with the thought. Well, he had paid back for Old Charlie, with interest. He grieved again for Isobel.

Finally he wondered about the orders, all the way from HQ, that had sent him to Sir Isaac. Was there actually a military job here? Or had Sir Isaac simply found out where he was and sent for him? The last seemed more likely; HQ would regard a request from a prince of the Egg as a military "must", dragons being as important as they were to operations.

He scratched the scar on his left arm and fell asleep.

Breakfast was as satisfactory as supper. This time there was no mystery about its appearance; it was wheeled in by a young dragon—Don knew that she was young as her rear pair of eyestalks were still buds; she could not have been more than a Venus century old. Don whistled his thanks; she answered politely and left.

Don wondered if Sir Isaac employed human servants; the cooking puzzled him—dragons simply do not cook. They prefer their fodder fresh, with a little of the bottom mud still clinging to it, for flavor. He could imagine a dragon boiling an egg the proper length of time, the time having been stated, but his imagination boggled at anything more complicated. Human cookery is an esoteric and strictly racial art.

His puzzlement did not keep him from enjoying breakfast.

After breakfast, his self-confidence shored up by clean and reasonably neat clothes, he braced himself for the ordeal of meeting Sir Isaac's numerous family. Used as he was to acting as a "true speech" interpreter the prospect of so much ceremoniousness in which he himself would be expected to play a central and imaginative part made him nervous. He hoped that he would be able to carry it off in a fashion that would reflect honor on his parents and not embarrass his sponsor.

He had shaved sketchily, having no mirror, and was ready to make his sortie, when he heard his name called. It surprised him, as he knew that he should not have been disturbed—being a guest freshly arrived—even if he chose to stay in his chambers for a week, or a month—or forever.

Sir Isaac lumbered in. "My dear boy, will you forgive an old man in a hurry for treating you with the informality ordinarily used only with one's own children?"

"Why, certainly, Sir Isaac." Don was still puzzled. If Sir Isaac were a dragon in a hurry, he was the first one in history.

"If you are refreshed, then please come with me." Don did so, reflecting that they must have had him under observation; Sir Isaac's entrance was too timely. The old dragon led him out of his chambers, down a passage, and into a room which might have been considered cozy by dragon standards; it was less than a hundred feet across.

Don decided that it must be Sir Isaac's study, as there were roll upon roll of ribbon books racked on the walls and

146

the usual sort of rotating bench set at the height of his handling tentacles. Above the racks on one wall was what Don judged to be a mural, but it looked like meaningless daubs to him; the three colors in the infra-red which dragons see and we do not produced the usual confusion. On second thought he decided that it might actually be meaningless; certainly a lot of human art did not seem to mean anything.

But the point which he noticed most and wondered about was that the room contained not one but two chairs meant for humans.

Sir Isaac invited him to sit down. Don did so and found that the chair was of the best powered furniture; it felt out his size and shape and conformed to it. He found out at once for whom the other terrestrial chair was intended; a man strode in—fiftyish, lean and hard in the belly, wiry grey hair around a bald pate. He had an abrupt manner and gave the impression that his orders were always obeyed. "Morning, gentlemen!" He turned to Don. "You're Don Harvey. My name's Phipps—Montgomery Phipps." He spoke as if that were sufficient explanation. "You've grown some. Last time I saw you I walloped your britches for biting my thumb."

Don felt put off by the man's top-sergeant air. He supposed that it was some acquaintance of his parents whom he had met in the dim reaches of his childhood, but he could not place him. "Did I have reason to bite it?" he asked.

"Eh?" The man suddenly gave a barking laugh. "I suppose that is a matter of opinion. But we were even; I spanked you properly." He turned to Sir Isaac. "Is Malath going to be here?"

"He told me that he would make the effort. He should be along shortly."

Phipps threw himself in the other chair and drummed on the arms of it. "Well, I suppose we must wait, though I don't see the need of his attending. There has been much too much delay now—we should have had this meeting last night."

Sir Isaac managed to drag a shocked tone out of his voder. "Last night? With a guest newly arrived?"

Phipps shrugged. "Never mind." He turned back to Don. "How did you like your dinner, son?"

"Very much."

"My wife cooked it. She's busy in the lab now, but you'll meet her later. Top flight chemist—in or out of the kitchen."

"I'd like to thank her," Don said sincerely. "Did you say 'lab'?"

"Eh? Yes, yes—quite a place. You'll see it later. Some of the best talent on Venus here. The Federation's loss is our gain."

The questions that immediately popped into Don's mind were held up; someone—something—was coming in. Don's eyes widened when he saw that it was a Martian's "pram"— the self-propelled personal environment without which a Martian cannot live either on Earth or Venus. The little car wheeled in and joined the circle; the figure inside raised itself to a sitting position with the aid of its powered artificial exoskeleton, tried feebly to spread its pseudowings and spoke, its thin, tired voice amplified through a speaking system. "Malath da Thon greets you, my friends."

Phipps stood up. "Malath, old boy, you should be back in your tank. You'll kill yourself exerting like this."

"I shall live as long as is necessary."

"Here's the Harvey kid. Looks like his old man, doesn't he?"

Sir Isaac, shocked by such casualness, intervened with a formal introduction. Don tried feverishly to recall more than two words of High Martian, gave up and let it go with, "I'm glad to know you, sir."

"The honor is mine," answered the tired voice. " 'A tall father casts a long shadow.' "

Don wondered what to answer while reflecting that the rowdy lack of manners of the move-overs had its points. Phipps broke in with, "Well, let's get down to business before Malath wears himself out. Sir Isaac?"

"Very well. Donald, you know that you are welcome in my house."

"Uh—why, yes, Sir Isaac, thank you."

"You know that I urged you to visit me before I knew aught of you but your parentage and your own good spirit."

"Yes, sir, you asked me to look you up. And I tried to, I really did—but I didn't know where you had landed. I was just getting organized to do a little detective work on it when the Greenies landed. I'm sorry." Don felt vaguely uncomfortable, knowing that he had put the matter off until he had a favor to ask.

"And I tried to find you, Donald—and was caught by the same mischance. Most recently, by rumors that are carried on the mist, did I discover where you were and what you were doing." Sir Isaac paused as if he found the choice of words difficult. "Knowing that this house is yours, knowing that you were welcome in any case, can you forgive me when you discover you were summoned also for a most practical reason?"

Don decided that this called for "true speech." " 'How can the eyes offend the tail? Or father offend son?' What can I do to help, Sir Isaac? I had already gathered that something was up."

"How shall I begin? Should I speak of your Cyrus Buchanan who died far from his people, yet died happily since he had made us his people, too? Or should I speak of the strange and complicated customs of your own people wherein you sometimes—or so it appears to us—cause the jaw to bite its own leg? Or should I discuss directly the events that have happened here since first you and I shared mud in the sky?"

Phipps stirred uneasily. "Let me handle it, Sir Isaac. Remember that this young man and I are of the same race. We won't have to beat around the bush; I can put it up to him in two words. It isn't complicated."

Sir Isaac lowered his massive head. "As you wish, my friend."

Phipps turned to Don. "Young fellow, you didn't know it, but when your parents called you home to Mars, you were a courier with a message."

Don looked at him sharply. "But I did know it." His mind raced ahead, adjusting himself to this new situation.

"You did? Well, that's fine! Let's have it, then."

"Have what?"

"The ring—the ring, of course. Give it to us."

XV

"Judge Not According to the Appearance"

JOHN VII:24

"WAIT a minute," Don protested. "You're mixed up. I know what ring you mean, all right, but it wasn't the ring; it was the paper that it was wrapped in. And the I.B.I. got that."

Phipps looked perplexed, then laughed. "They did, eh? Then they made the same mistake you did. But it's the ring itself that is important. Let's have it."

"You must be mistaken," Don answered slowly. "Or maybe we aren't talking about the same ring." He thought about it. "It's possible that the I.B.I. swapped rings before the package ever reached me. But it's a dead cinch that the ring that was delivered to me couldn't have contained a message. It was transparent plastic—styrene, probably—and there wasn't even a fly speck in it. No message. No way to hide a message."

Phipps shrugged impatiently. "Don't quibble with me as to whether or not a message could be concealed in the ring—it's the right ring; be sure of that. The I.B.I. didn't switch rings—we *know*."

"How do you know?"

"Confound it, boy! Your function was to deliver the ring, that's all. You let us worry about the message in it."

Don was beginning to feel sure that when his younger self had bitten Phipps' thumb, he must have been justified. "Wait a minute! I was to deliver the ring, yes—that is what Dr. Jefferson—you know who he is?"

"I knew who he was. I've never met him."

"That's what Dr. Jefferson wanted. He's dead, or so they told me. In any case I can't consult him. But he was very specific about *to whom* I was to deliver it—to my father. Not to you."

Phipps pounded the arm of the chair. "I know it, I know it! If things had gone properly, you would have delivered it to your father and we would have been saved no end of trouble. But those eager lads in New London had to— Never mind. The rebellion occurring when it did caused you to wind up here instead of on Mars. I'm trying to pick up the pieces. You can't deliver it to your father, but you can get the same result by turning it over to me. Your father and I are working toward the same end."

Don hesitated before answering, "I don't wish to be rude —but you ought to give some proof of that."

Sir Isaac produced with his voder a sound exactly like a man clearing his throat. "Ahem!" They both turned their heads toward him. "Perhaps," he went on, "I should enter the discussion. I have known Donald, if I may say so, more recently, my dear Phipps."

"Well—go ahead."

Sir Isaac turned most of his eyes on Don. "My dear Donald, do you trust me?"

"Uh, I think so, Sir Isaac—but it seems to me that I am obligated to insist on proof. It isn't my ring."

"Yes, you have reason. Then let us consider what would be proof. If I say——"

Don interrupted, feeling that the whole matter was out of hand. "I'm sorry I let this grow into an argument. You see, it does not matter."

"Eh?"

"Well, you see, I don't have the ring any longer. It's gone."

There was a dead silence for a long minute. Then Phipps said, "I think Malath has fainted."

There was scurrying excitement while the Martian's cart was removed to his chambers, tension until it was reported that he was floating in his very special bed and resting comfortably. The conference resumed with three members. Phipps glowered at Don. "It's your fault, you know. What you said took the heart out of him."

"Me? I don't understand."

"He was a courier, too—he was stranded here the same way you were. He has the other half of the message—of the message you lost. And you removed the last possible chance he has of getting home before high gravity kills him. He's a sick man—and you jerked the rug out from under him."

Donald said, "But——"

Sir Isaac interrupted. "Donald is not at fault. The young should be blamed only with just cause and after deliberation, lest the family sorrow."

Phipps glanced at the dragon, then back at Don. "I'm sorry. I'm tired and bad tempered. What's done is done. The important point is: what happened to the ring? Is there any possibility of locating it?"

Don looked unhappy. "I'm afraid not." He explained rapidly about the attempt to get the ring from him and how he had had no proper place to protect it. "I didn't know that it was really important but I was determined to carry out Dr. Jefferson's wishes—maybe I'm sort of stubborn at times. So I did the best I could think of to do; I turned it over to a friend for safekeeping. I figured that was best because no one would think of looking for it in the hands of a person who wouldn't be expected to have it."

"Sound enough," agreed Phipps, "but to whom did you give it?"

"A young lady." Don's features contorted. "I think she was killed when the Greenies attacked."

"You don't know?"

"I'm fairly certain. I've been doing work that gives me opportunities to ask—and nobody has laid eyes on her since the attack. I'm sure she's dead."

"You could be wrong. What was her name?"

"Isobel Costello. Her father managed the I. T. & T. branch."

Phipps looked utterly astounded, then lay back in his chair and roared. Presently he wiped his eyes and said, "Did you hear that, Sir Isaac? Did you hear that? Talk about the Blue Bird in your own back yard! Talk about Grandma's spectacles!"

Don looked from one to the other. "What do you mean?" he asked in offended tones.

"What do I mean? Why, son, Jim Costello and his daughter have been right here since two days after the attack." He jumped out of his chair. "Don't move! Stay where you are—I'll be right back."

And he was back quickly. "I always have trouble with those funny house phones of yours, Sir Ike," he complained. "But they're coming." He sat down and heaved a sigh. "Some days I'm tempted to turn myself in as an idiot."

Phipps shut up, save for a suppressed chuckle or two. Sir Isaac seemed to be contemplating his non-existent navel. Don was preoccupied with turbulent thoughts, relief too great to be pleasure. Isobel alive!

Presently, calm somewhat restored, he spoke up. "Look— isn't it about time somebody told me what this is all about?"

Sir Isaac lifted his head and his tendrils played over the keys. "Your pardon, dear boy. I was thinking of something else. Long, long ago when my race was young and when your race had not yet——"

Phipps cut in. "Excuse me, old boy, but I can brief it and you can fill him in on the details later." He assumed assent and turned to Don. "Harvey, there is an organization—a cabal, a conspiracy, a secret lodge, call it what you like—we just call it 'The Organization'. I'm a member, so is Sir Isaac, so is old Malath—and so are both of your parents. And so was Dr. Jefferson. It's made up mostly of scientists but it is not limited to them; the one thing we all have in common is a belief in the dignity and natural worth of free intelligence. In many different ways we have fought— and fought unsuccessfully, I should add—against the historical imperative of the last two centuries, the withering away of individual freedom under larger and even more pervasive organizations, both governmental and quasi-governmental.

"On Earth our group derives from dozens of sources, 'way back in history—associations of scientists fighting against secrecy and the straitjacketing of thought, artists fighting against censorshop, legal aid societies, many other organizations, most of them unsuccessful, and some downright stupid. About a century ago all such things were pushed underground; the weak sisters dropped out, the talkative got themselves arrested and liquidated—and the remnants consolidated.

"Here on Venus our origins go clear back to the rapprochement between Cyrus Buchanan and the dominant natives. On Mars, in addition to many humans—more about them later—the organization is affiliated with what we call the 'priest class'—a bad translation, for they aren't priests; 'judges' would be closer."

Sir Isaac interrupted. " 'Elder brothers.' "

"Eh? Well, maybe that is a fair poetical rendering. Never mind. The point is, the whole organization, Martian, Venerian, Terrestrial, has been striving——"

"Just a minute," put in Don. "If you can answer me one question, it would clear up a whole lot. I'm a soldier of the Venus Republic and we've got a war on. Tell me this: is this organization—here on Venus, I mean—helping in our fight to chuck the Greenies out?"

"Well, not precisely. You see——"

Don did not then find out what it was he was supposed to see; another voice cut through Phipps' words: "Don! Donald!"

He found himself swarmed by a somewhat smaller and female member of his own race. Isobel seemed determined to break his neck. Don was embarrassed and upset and most happy. He gently removed her arms from his neck and tried to pretend that it had not happened—when he caught sight of her father looking at him quite oddly. "Uh, hello, Mr. Costello."

Costello advanced and shook hands with him. "How do you do, Mr. Harvey? It's good to see you again."

"It's good to see you. I'm mighty glad to see you folks alive and in one piece. I thought you had had it."

"Not quite. But it was a near thing."

Isobel said, "Don, you look older—much older. And how thin you are!"

He grinned at her. "You look just the same, Grandma."

Phipps interrupted, "Much as I dislike breaking up Old

Home Week we have no time to waste. Miss Costello, we want the ring."

"The ring?"

"He means," explained Don, "the ring I left with you."

"Ring?" said Mr. Costello. "Mr. Harvey, did you give my daughter a ring?"

"Well, not exactly. You see——"

Phipps interrupted again. "It's *the* ring, Jim—the message ring. Harvey was the other courier—and it seems he made your daughter sort of a deputy courier."

"Eh? I must say I'm confused." He looked at his daughter.

"You have it?" Don asked her. "You didn't lose it?"

"Lose your ring? Of course not, Don. But I had thought—Never mind; you want it back now." She glanced around at the eyes on her—fourteen, counting Sir Isaac's—then moved away and turned her back. She turned around again almost immediately and held out her hand. "Here it is."

Phipps reached for it. Isobel drew her hand away and handed it to Don. Phipps opened his mouth, closed it again, then reopened it. "Very well—now let's have it, Harvey."

Don put it in a pocket. "You never did get around to explaining why I should turn it over to you."

"But—" Phipps turned quite red. "This is preposterous! Had we known it was here, we would never have bothered to send for you—we would have had it without your leave."

"Oh, no!"

Phipps swung his eyes to Isobel. "What's that, young lady? Why not?"

"Because I wouldn't have given it to you—not ever. Don *told* me that someone was trying to get it away from him. I didn't know that *you* were the one!"

Phipps, already red-faced, got almost apoplectic. "I've had all this childish kidding around with serious matters that I can stand." He took two long strides to Don and grasped him by the arm. "Cut out the nonsense and give us that message!"

Don shook him off and backed away half a step, all in one smooth motion—and Phipps looked down to see the point of a blade almost touching his waistband. Don held the knife with the relaxed thumb-and-two-finger grip of those who understand steel.

Phipps seemed to have trouble believing what he saw. Don said to him softly, "Get away from me."

Phipps backed away. "Sir Isaac!"

"Yes," agreed Don. "Sir Isaac—do I have to put up with this in your house?"

The dragon's tentacles struck the keys, but only confused squawking came out. He stopped and started again and said very slowly, "Donald—this is your house. You are always safe in it. Please—by the service you did me—put away your weapon."

Don glanced at Phipps, straightened up and caused his knife to disappear. Phipps relaxed and turned to the dragon. "Well, Sir Isaac? What are you going to do about it?"

Sir Isaac did not bother with the voder. "*Remove thyself!*"

"Eh?"

"You have brought dissension into this house. Were you not both in my house and of my family? Yet you menaced him. Please go—before you cause more sorrow."

Phipps started to speak, thought better of it—left. Don said, "Sir Isaac, I am terribly sorry. I——"

"Let the waters close over it. Let the mud bury it. Donald, my dear boy, how can I assure you that what we ask of you is what your honored parents would have you do, were they here to instruct you?"

Don considered this. "I think that's just the trouble, Sir Isaac—I'm not your 'dear boy.' I'm not anybody's 'dear boy.' My parents aren't here and I'm not sure that I would let them instruct me if they were. I'm a grown man now—I'm not as old as you are, not by several centuries. I'm not very old even by human standards—Mr. Phipps still classes me as a boy and that was what was wrong. But I'm not a boy and I've got to know what's going on and make up my own mind. So far, I've heard a lot of sales talk and I've been subjected to a lot of verbal pushing around. That won't do; I've got to know the real facts."

Before Sir Isaac could reply they were interrupted by another sound—Isobel was applauding. Don said to her. "How about you, Isobel? What do you know about all this?"

"Me? Nothing. I couldn't be more in the dark if I were stuffed in a sack. I was just cheering your sentiments."

"My daughter," Mr. Costello put in crisply, "knows nothing at all of these things. But I do—and it appears that you are entitled to answers."

"I could certainly use some!"

"By your leave, Sir Isaac?" The dragon ponderously inclined his head; Costello went on, "Fire away. I'll try to give you straight answers."

"Okay—what's the message in the ring?"

"Well, I can't answer that exactly or we wouldn't need the message ourselves. I know that it's a discussion of certain aspects of physics—gravitation and inertia and spin and things like that. Field theory. It's certainly very long and very complicated and I probably wouldn't understand it if I knew exactly what was in it. I'm simply a somewhat rusty communications engineer, not a topflight theoretical physicist."

Don looked puzzled. "I don't get it. Somebody tucks a physics book into a ring—and then we play cops-and-robbers all around the system. It sounds silly. Furthermore, it sounds impossible." He took the ring out and looked at it; the light shone through it clearly. It was just a notions counter trinket—how could a major work on physics be hidden in it?

Sir Isaac said, "Donald, my dear— I beg pardon. Shucks! You mistake simple appearance for simplicity. Be assured; it is in there. It is theoretically possible to have a matrix in which each individual molecule has a meaning—as they do in the memory cells of your brain. If we had such subtlety, we could wrap your Encyclopedia Britannica into the head of a pin—it would *be* the head of that pin. But this is nothing so difficult."

Don looked again at the ring and put it back in his pocket. "Okay, if you say so. But I still don't see what all the shooting is about."

Mr. Costello answered, "We don't either—not exactly. This message was intended to go to Mars, where they are prepared to make the best use of it. I myself had not even heard about the project except in the most general terms until I was brought here. But the main idea is this: the equations that are included in this message tell how space is put together—and how to manipulate it. I can't even imagine all the implications of that—but we do know a couple of things that we expect from it, first, how to make a force field that will stop anything, even a fusion bomb, and second, how to hook up a space drive that would make rocket travel look like walking. Don't ask me how—I'm out of my depth. Ask Sir Isaac."

"Ask me after I've studied the message," the dragon commented dryly.

Don made no comment. There was silence for some moments which Costello broke by saying, "Well? Do you want to ask anything? I do not know quite what you do know; I hardly know what to volunteer."

"Mr. Costello, when I talked to you in New London, did you know about this message?"

Costello shook his head. "I knew that our organization had great hopes from an investigation going on on Earth. I knew that it was intended to finish on Mars—you see, I was the key man, the 'drop box,' for communication to and from Venus, because I was in a position to handle interplanetary messages. I did not know that you were a courier—and I certainly did not know that you had entrusted an organization message to my only daughter." He smiled wryly. "I might add that I did not even identify you in my mind as the son of two members of our organization, else there would have been no question about handling your traffic whether you could pay for it or not. There were means whereby I could spot organization messages—identifications that your message lacked. And Harvey is a fairly common name."

"You know," Don said slowly, "it seems to me that if Dr. Jefferson had told me what it was I was carrying—and if you had trusted Isobel here with some idea of what was going on, a lot of trouble could have been saved."

"Perhaps. But men have died for knowing too much. Conversely, what they don't know they can't tell."

"Yes, I suppose so. But there ought to be some way

of running things so that people don't have to go around loaded with secrets and afraid to speak!"

Both the dragon and the man inclined their heads. Mr. Costello added, "That's exactly what we're after—in the long run. That sort of a world."

Don turned to his host. "Sir Isaac, when we met in the *Glory Road*, did you know that Dr. Jefferson was using me as a messenger?"

"No, Donald—though I should have suspected it when I learned who you were." He paused, then added, "Is there anything more you wish to know?"

"No, I just want to think." Too many things had happened too fast, too many new ideas— Take what Mr. Costello had said about what was in the ring, now—he could see what that would mean—if Costello knew what he was talking about. A fast space drive, one that would run rings around the Federation ships . . . a way to guard against atom bombs, even fusion bombs—why, if the Republic had such things they could tell the Federation to go fly a kite!

But that so-and-so Phipps had admitted that all this hanky-panky was not for the purpose of fighting the Greenies. They wanted to send the stuff to Mars, whatever it was. Why Mars? Mars didn't even have a permanent human settlement—just scientific commissions and expeditions, like the work his parents did. The place wasn't fit for humans, not really. So why Mars?

Whom could he trust? Isobel, of course—he had trusted her and it had paid off. Her father? Isobel and her father were two different people and Isobel didn't know anything about what her father was doing. He looked at her; she stared back with big, serious eyes. He looked at her father. He didn't know, he just didn't know.

Malath? A voice out of a tank! Phipps? Phipps might be kind to children and have a heart of gold, but Don had no reason to trust him.

To be sure, all these people knew about Dr. Jefferson, knew about the ring, seemed to know about his parents—but so had Bankfield. He needed *proof*, not words. He knew enough now, enough had happened now, to prove to him that what he carried was of utmost importance. He *must not* make a mistake.

It occurred to him that there was one possible way of checking: Phipps had told him that Malath carried the other half of the same message—that the ring carried only one half. If it turned out that his half fitted the part that Malath carried, it would pretty well prove that these people had a right to the message.

But, confound it all!—that test required him to break the egg to discover that it was bad. He had to know *before* he turned it over to them. He had met the two-piece message system before; it was a standard military dodge—but used and used *only* when it was so terribly, terribly important not to let a message be compromised that you would rather not have it delivered than take any risk at all of having it fall into the wrong hands.

He looked up at the dragon. "Sir Isaac?"

"Yes, Donald?"

"What would happen if I refused to give up the ring?"

Sir Isaac answered at once but with grave deliberation. "You are my own egg, no matter what. This is your house—where you may dwell in peace—or leave in peace—as is your will."

"*Thank you, Sir Isaac.*" Don trilled it in dragon symbols and used "Sir Isaac's" true name.

Costello said urgently, "Mr. Harvey——"

"Yes?"

"Do you know *why* the speech of the dragon people is called 'true speech'?"

"Uh, why, no, not exactly."

"Because it *is* true speech. See here—I've studied comparative semantics—the whistling talk does not even contain a symbol for the concept of falsehood. *And what a person does not have symbols for he can't think about!* Ask him, Mr. Harvey! Ask him *in his own speech*. If he answers at all, you can believe him."

Donald looked at the old dragon. The thought went racing through his mind that Costello was right—there was no symbol in dragon speech for "lie," the dragons apparently never had arrived at the idea—or the need. Could Sir Isaac tell a lie? Or was he so far humanized that he could behave and think like a man? He stared at Sir Isaac and eight blank, oscillating eyes looked back at him. How could a man know what a dragon was thinking?

"Ask him!" insisted Costello.

He didn't trust Phipps; he couldn't logically trust Costello—he had no reason to. And Isobel didn't figure into it. But a man had to trust somebody, some time! A man couldn't go it alone—all right, let it be this dragon who had "shared mud" with him. "It isn't necessary," Don said suddenly. "Here." He reached into his pocket, took out the ring and slipped it over one of Sir Isaac's tentacles.

The tentacle curled through it and withdrew it into the slowly writhing mass. *"I thank you, Mist-on-the-Waters."*

XVI

Multum in Parvo

DONALD looked at Isobel and found her still solemn, unsmiling, but she seemed to show approval. Her father sat down heavily in the other chair. "Phew!" he sighed. "Mr. Harvey, you are a hard nut. You had me worried."

"I'm sorry. I had to think."

"No matter now." He turned to Sir Isaac. "I guess I had better dig up Phipps. Yes?"

"It won't be necessary." The voice came from behind them; they all turned—all but Sir Isaac who did not need to turn his body. Phipps stood just inside the door. "I came in on the tail end of your remark, Jim. If you want me, I'm here."

"Well, yes."

"Just a moment, then. I came for another reason." He faced Don. "Mr. Harvey, I owe you an apology."

"Oh, that's all right."

"No, let me say my say. I had no business trying to bullyrag you into cooperating. Don't mistake me; we want that ring—we *must* have it. And I mean to argue until we get it. But I've been under great strain and I went about it the wrong way. Very great strain—that's my only excuse."

"Well," said Don, "come to think about it, so have I. So let's forget it." He turned to his host. "Sir Isaac, may I?" He reached toward Sir Isaac's handling tentacles, putting out his palm. The ring dropped into it; he turned and handed it to Phipps.

Phipps stared at it stupidly for a moment. When he looked up Don was surprised to see that the man's eyes were filled with tears. "I won't thank you," he said, "because when you see what will come of this it will mean more to you than any person's thanks. What is in this ring is of life and death importance to many, many people. You'll see."

Don was embarrassed by the man's naked emotion. "I can guess," he said gruffly. "Mr. Costello told me that it meant bomb protection and faster ships—and I bet on my hunch that you people and I are on the same side in the long run. I just hope I didn't guess wrong."

"Guess wrong? No, you haven't guessed wrong—and not just in the long run, as you put it, but *right now!* Now that we have this—" he held up the ring, "we stand a fighting chance to save our people on Mars."

"Mars?" repeated Don. "Hey, wait a minute—what's this about Mars? Who's going to be saved? And from what?"

Phipps looked just as puzzled. "Eh? But wasn't that what persuaded you to turn over the ring?"

"Wasn't *what* persuaded me?"

"Didn't Jim Costello—" "Why, I thought of course you had—" and Sir Isaac's voder interrupted with, "Gentlemen, apparently it was assumed that——"

"*Quiet!*" Don shouted. As Phipps opened his mouth again Don hurriedly added, "Things seem to have gotten mixed up again. Can somebody—just one of you—tell me what goes on?"

Costello could and did. The Organization had for many years been quietly building a research center on Mars. It was the one place in the system where the majority of humans were scientists. The Federation maintained merely an outpost there, with a skeleton garrison. Mars was not regarded as being of any real importance—just a place where harmless longhairs could dig among the ruins and study the customs of the ancient and dying race.

The security officers of the I.B.I. gave Mars little attention; there seemed no need. The occasional agent who did show up could be led around and allowed to see research of no military importance.

The group on Mars did not have the giant facilities available on Earth—the mastodonic cybernetic machines, the unlimited sources of atomic power, the superpowerful particle accelerators, the enormous laboratories—but they did have freedom. The theoretical ground-work for new advances in physics had been worked out on Mars, spurred on by certain mystifying records of the First Empire—that almost mythical earlier epoch when the solar system had been one political unit. Don was warmly pleased, to hear that his parents' researches had contributed largely at this point in the problem. It was known—or so the ancient Martian records seemed to state—that the ships of the First Empire had traveled between the planets, not in journeys of weary months, or even weeks, but of *days*.

The descriptions of these ships and of their motive power were extensive, but differences in language, in concept, and in technology created obstacles enough to give comparative semanticists nervous breakdowns—had done so, in fact. A treatise on modern electronics written in Sanskrit poetry with half the thoughts taken for granted would have been lucid in comparison.

It had simply been impossible to make fully intelligible translation of the ancient records. What was missing had to be worked out by genius and sweat.

When the theoretical work had been carried as far as it could be the problem was sent to Earth via members of the Organization for *sub rosa* testing and for conversion of theory into present-day engineering. At first there was a steady traffic of information back and forth between planets, but, as the secret grew, the members of the Organization were less and less inclined to travel for fear of compromising what they knew. By the time of the Venus crisis it had been standard practice for some years to send critical information by couriers who knew nothing and therefore could not talk—such as Don—or by non-terrestrials who were physically immune to the interrogation methods of the security police—giving a Venerian dragon the "third degree" was not only impractical, but ridiculous. For different but equally obvious reasons Martians too were safe from the thought police.

Don himself was a last-minute choice, a "channel of opportunity"—the Venus crisis had rushed things. How badly it had rushed things no one knew until after Commodore Higgins' spectacular raid on Circum-Terra. The engineering data so urgently needed on Mars had gone to Venus instead, there to be lost (Don's half of it) in the confusion of rebellion and counterblow. The rebelling colonists, driving toward the same goal as the Organization, had unknowingly thwarted their best chance for overthrowing the Federation.

Communication between the Organization members on Venus, on Earth, and on Mars had been precariously and imperfectly reestablished right under the noses of the Federation police. The Organization had members working for I. T. & T. on all three planets—members such as Costello. Costello himself had been helped to make his escape, with Isobel, because he knew too much; they could not afford to have him questioned—but a new "drop box" had been set up at Governor's Island in the person of a Federation communications technical sergeant. The channel to the sergeant was a dragon who had the garbage disposal contract for the "Greenie" base. The dragon had no voder; the sergeant knew no whistle talk—but a tentacle can pass a note to a human hand.

Communication, though difficult and dangerous, was possible; travel between planets for members of the Organization was now utterly impossible. The only commercial line as yet reestablished was the Earth-Moon run. The group on Venus was attempting the almost impossible task of completing a project all preliminary preparations for which had been made for Mars. The task was not quite impossible—provided they could find the missing half of the message, they might yet outfit a ship, send it to Mars, and finish the job.

So they hoped . . . and continued to hope until recently, when disastrous news had gotten through to them from Earth—the Organization had been penetrated on Earth; a very senior member, one who knew much too much, had been arrested and had not been able to suicide in time.

And a task force of Federation ships was already on its way to attack the group on Mars.

"Wait a minute!" Don interrupted. "I thought—Mr. Costello, didn't you tell me, back in New London, that the Federation had already moved in on Mars?"

"Not exactly. I told you that I had inferred that the Federation had taken over Schiaparelli Station, the I. T. & T. branch there. And so they had—to the extent of censoring all traffic and putting a stop to all traffic with Venus. They could do that with a squad of soldiers from the pint-sized garrison they've always had there. But this is an attack in force. They mean to liquidate the Organization."

Liquidate the Organization—Don translated the jawbreakers into real words: kill all the people who were against them. That meant his parents—

He shook his head to clear it. The thought did not mean anything to him inside. It had been too many years; he could not see their faces—and he could not imagine them dead. He wondered if he himself had become dead inside, unable to feel things. No matter—something had to be done. "What do we do? How can we stop it?"

"We quit wasting time!" answered Phipps. "We've lost half a day already. Sir Isaac?"

"Yes, my friend. Let us hurry."

The room was a laboratory shop, but of dragon proportions. It needed to be, for it held a round dozen of dragons as well as fifty-odd men and a sprinkling of women. Everyone who could manage it wanted to see the opening of the ring. Even Malath da Thon was there, sitting up in his cell with the aid of his power-driven corset and with the colors of emotion rippling gently across his frail body.

Don and Isobel had climbed to the top of the entrance ramp, where they could see without being in the way. Opposite them was a large stereo tank, lighted but with no picture growing in it. Below them was a micromanipulator, dragon style; other pieces of apparatus and power tools filled the rest of the room. They were strange to Don, not because they were of dragon construction and for dragon use, for many of them were not—they were strange in the way in which laboratory equipment is always exotic to the layman. He was used to dragon artifacts; the two technologies, human and dragon, had interpenetrated sufficiently that a human, especially one living on Venus, found nothing odd in joints that were wrung instead of welded or bolted, nothing unusual in interlocking ovoids where a man would use screws.

Sir Isaac was at the micromanipulator, his tendrils at the controls; down over his head fitted a frame with eight eyepieces. He touched the control rack; the tank rippled and a picture built in it—the ring, in full color and three dimensions. It seemed to be about eight feet across. The boss of the ring faced out, displaying the enamel-filled initial cut into it—a capital "H" framed with a simple circle of white enamel.

The picture flickered and changed. Only a portion of the initial was now visible, but so greatly magnified that the enamel rubbed into the shallow grooves of the letter looked like broken paving blocks. A shadowy pointed cylinder, out of focus save at its very end, moved across the picture; a great oily globe formed on the end of it, detached itself and settled on the enamel. The "paving blocks" started to break up.

Montgomery Phipps climbed the ramp, saw Don and Isobel, and sat down on the edge beside them. He seemed to want to be friendly. "This will be something to tell your grandchildren about," he remarked. "Old Sir Ike at work. The best microtechnician in the system—can darn near pick out a single molecule, make it sit up and beg."

"It rather surprises me," Don admitted. "I hadn't known that Sir Isaac was a laboratory technician."

"He's more than that; he's a great physicist; hadn't the significance of his chosen name struck you?"

Don felt foolish. He knew how dragons went about picking vocalized names, but he took such names for granted, just as he took his own Venerian name for granted. "His whole tribe tends to be scientific," Phipps went on. "There's a grandson who calls himself 'Galileo Galilei'; have you met him? And there's a 'Doctor Einstein' and a 'Madame Curie' and there's an integrating chemist who calls herself— Egg alone knows why!—'Little Buttercup.' But old Sir Ike is the boss man, the top brain—he made a trip to Earth to help with some of the work on this project. But you knew that, didn't you?"

Donald admitted that he had not known why Sir Isaac was on Earth. Isobel put in, "Mr. Phipps, if Sir Isaac was working on this on Earth, why doesn't he know what is in the ring before he opens it?"

"Well, he does and he doesn't. He worked on the theoretical end. But what we will find—unless we get a terrific disappointment—will be detailed engineering instructions worked out for man-type tools and techniques. Very different."

Don thought about it. "Engineering" and "science" were more or less lumped together in his mind; he lacked the training to appreciate the enormous difference. He changed the subject. "You are a laboratory man yourself, Mr. Phipps?"

"Me? Heavens, no! My fingers are all thumbs. The dynamics of history is my game. Theoretical once—applied now. Well, that's a dry hole." His eyes were on the tank; the solvent, sluiced in by what seemed to be hogshead amounts, had washed the enamel out of the groove that defined that part of the initial "H"; the floor of the groove could be seen, bare, amber, and transparent.

Phipps stood up. "I can't sit still—I get nervous. Excuse me, please."

"Surely."

A dragon was lumbering up the ramp. He stopped by them just as Phipps was turning away. "Howdy, Mr. Phipps. Mind if I park here?"

167

"Not at all. Know these people?"

"I've met the lady."

Don acknowledged the introduction, giving both his names and receiving those of the dragon in turn—*Refreshing Rain* and Josephus ("Just call me 'Joe' "). Joe was the first dragon, other than Sir Isaac, whom Don had met there who was voder trained and equipped; Don looked at him with interest. One thing was certain: Joe had learned English from some master other than the nameless Cockney who had taught Sir Isaac . . . a Texan, Don felt quite sure.

"I am honored to be in your house," Don said to him.

The dragon settled himself comfortably, letting his chin come about to their shoulders. "Not my house. These snobs wouldn't have me around if there wasn't a job I can do a little better than the next hombre. I just work here."

"Oh." Don wanted to defend Sir Isaac against the charge of snobbery but taking sides between dragons seemed unwise. He looked back at the tank. The scan had shifted to the circle of enamel which framed the "H"; fifteen or twenty degrees of it appeared in the tank. The magnification started to swell enormously until one tiny sector filled the huge picture. Again the solvent floated into the enamel; again it washed away.

"Now we are getting someplace, maybe," commented Joe.

The enamel was dissolving like snow in spring rain, but, instead of washing down to a bare floor, something dark was revealed under the paint—a bundle of steel pipes, it seemed to be, nested in the shallow groove.

There was dead silence—then somebody cheered. Don found that he had been holding his breath. "What is it?" he asked Joe.

"Wire. What would you expect?"

Sir Isaac stepped up the magnification and shifted to another sector. Slowly, as carefully as a mother bathing her first born, he washed the covering off the upper layer of the coiled wire. Presently a microscopic claw reached in, felt around most delicately, and extracted one end.

Joe got to his feet. "Got to get to work," he keyed. "That's my cue." He ambled down the ramp. Don noticed that he was growing a new starboard-midships leg and the process was not quite complete; it gave him a lopsided, one-flat-wheel gait.

Slowly, tenderly, the wire was cleaned and uncoiled. More than an hour later the tiny hands of the micromanipulator stretched out their prize—four feet of steel wire so gossamer fine that it could not be seen at all by naked eye, even by a dragon.

Sir Isaac backed his head out of the eyepiece rack. "Is Malath's wire ready?" he inquired.

"All set."

"Very well, my friends. Let us commence."

They were fed into two ordinary microwire speakers, rigged in parallel. Seated at a control panel for synchronizing the fragmented message latent in the two wires was a worried-looking man wearing earphones—Mr. Costello. The steel spider threads started very slowly through—and a high-pitched gabbling came out of the horn. There were very rapid momentary interruptions, like high frequency code.

"Not in synch," announced Mr. Costello. "Rewind."

An operator sitting in front of him said, "I hate to rewind, Jim. These wires would snap if you breathed on them."

"So you break a wire—Sir Isaac will splice it. Rewind!"

"Maybe you've got one in backwards."

"Shut up and rewind."

Presently the gabbling resumed. To Don it sounded the same as before and utterly meaningless, but Mr. Costello nodded. "That's got it. Was it recorded from the beginning?"

Don heard Joe's Texas accents answering, "In the can!"

"Okay, keep it rolling and start playing back the recording. Try slowing the composite twenty to one." Costello threw a switch; the gabbling stopped completely although the machines continued to unreel the invisible threads. Shortly a human voice came out of the loudspeaker horn; it was deep, muffled, dragging, and almost unintelligible. Joe stopped it and made an adjustment, started over. When the voice resumed it was a clear, pleasant, most careful enunciated contralto.

"Title," the voice said, " 'Some Notes on the Practical Applications of the Horst-Milne Equations. Table of Contents: Part One—On the Design of Generators to Accomplish Strain-

Free Molar Translation. Part Two—The Generation of Space-Time Discontinuities, Closed, Open, and Folded. Part Three —On the Generation of Temporary Pseudo-Acceleration Loci. Part One, Chapter One—Design Criteria for a Simple Generator and Control System. Referring to equation seventeen in Appendix A, it will be seen that—' "

The voice flowed on and on, apparently tireless. Don was interested, intensely so, but he did not understand it. He found himself growing sleepy when the voice suddenly rapped out: "Facsimile! Facsimile! Facsimile!"

Costello touched a switch, stopping the voice, and demanded, "Cameras ready?"

"Hot and rolling!"

"*Shift!*"

They watched the picture build up—a wiring diagram, Don decided it must be—or else a plate of spaghatti. When the picture was complete the voice resumed.

After more than two hours of this, broken only by desultory conversation, Don turned to Isobel. "I'm not doing any good here and I'm certainly not learning anything. What do you say we leave?"

"Suits."

They went down the ramp and headed for a tunnel that led toward living quarters. On the way they ran into Phipps, his face glowing with happiness. Don nodded and started to push on past; Phipps stopped him. "I was just going to hunt you up."

"Me?"

"Yes. I thought you might want this—for a souvenir." He held out the ring.

Don took it and examined it curiously. There was a very tiny break in one branch of the "H" where the enamel had been eaten away. The framing circle was an empty, slightly shadowed groove, a groove so narrow and shallow that Don could hardly catch his fingernail in it.

"You've no more use for it?"

"It's squeezed dry. Keep it. You'll be able to sell it to a museum some day, for a high price."

"No," said Don. "I reckon I'll deliver it to my father—eventually."

XVII

To Reset the Clock

DON moved out of the Gargantuan chambers he had been given and in with the other humans. Sir Isaac would have let him stay until the Sun grew cold, monopolizing an acre or so of living space, but to Don it seemed not only silly for one person to clutter up chambers built big enough for dragons but not entirely comfortable—so much open space made a man tuned to bush fighting uneasy.

The human guests occupied one dragon apartment with the great rooms partitioned off into cubicles. They shared its wallowing trough as a plunge bath and had a communal mess. Don roomed with Dr. Roger Conrad, a tall and shaggy young man with a perpetual grin. Don was a bit surprised to find that Conrad was held in high esteem by the other scientists.

He saw very little of his roommate, nor of any of the others—even Isobel was busy with clerical work. The team worked night and day with driving intensity. The ring had been opened and they had engineering data to work from, true—but that task force was already swinging toward Mars. Nobody knew—nobody *could* know—whether or not they could finish in time to save their colleagues.

Conrad had tried to explain it to Don one night late as he was turning in. "We don't have adequate facilities here. The instructions were conceived in terms of Earth- and Mars-type techniques. The dragons do things differently. We've got mighty little of our own stuff and it's hard to jury-rig what we need from their stuff. The original notion was to install the gear in—you know those little jumpbug ships that people use to get around in on Mars?"

"Seen pictures of them."

"Never actually seen 'em myself. Useless as rocketships, of course, but they are pressurized and big enough. Now we've got to adapt for a shuttle." A superstratospheric shuttle "with its ears trimmed"—the spreading glider wings unshipped and carried away—waited in a covered bayou outside Sir Isaac's family seat. It would make the trip to Mars—if it could be prepared. "It's a headache," he added.

"Well, can we do it?"

"We'll *have* to do it. We can't possibly do the design calculations over again; we don't have the machines, even if we had time to re-engineer the job—which we haven't."

"That's what I meant. Will you finish in time?"

Conrad sighed. "I wish I knew."

The pressure of time sat heavily on all of them. In their mess hall they had set up a large chart showing Earth, Sun, Venus, and Mars, each in its proper position. At lunch each day the markers were moved along the scribed orbits, the Earth by one degree, Venus a bit more, Mars by only half a degree and a trifle.

A long dotted line curved from a point on Earth's orbit to a rendezvous with Mars—their best estimate of the path and arrival date of the Federation task force. The departure date was all they knew with certainty; the trajectory itself and the arrival date were based on the relative positions of the two planets and what was believed to be the maximum performance of any Federation ship, assuming refueling in parking orbit around Earth.

For a rocket ship some orbits are possible, some are impossible. A military ship in a hurry would not, of course, use the economical doubly-tangent ellipse; such a trip, Earth to Mars would require 258 Earth days. But, even using hyperboloids and wasting fuel, there are severe limits to how quickly a reaction-driven ship can make an interplanetary voyage.

An Earth calendar hung beside the chart; near it was a clock showing Earth-Greenwich time. Posted near these was a figure, changed each time the clock read twenty-four hundred, the number of days till M-day—by their best estimate, now only thirty-nine.

Don was enjoying a combat soldier's paradise—hot food sharp on the hour, well cooked and plenty of it, all the sack time he cared to soak up, clean clothes, clean skin, no duties and no hazards. The only trouble was that he soon grew to hate it.

The intense activity around him shamed him into wanting to help—and try to help he did—until he found out that he was being given make-work to shut him up. Actually there was nothing he could do to help; the sweating specialists, trying their level best to haywire improbable circuits into working, had no time to waste on an untrained assistant. He gave up and went back to loafing, found that he could sleep all right in the afternoons but that the practice kept him awake at night.

He wondered why he could not enjoy so pleasant a leave. It was not that he was worried about his parents—

Yes, he was! Though they had grown dim in his memory his conscience was biting him that he was doing nothing helpful for them. That was why he wanted to get out, away from here where he could do no good, back to his outfit, back to his trade—back to where there was nothing to worry about between scrambles—and plenty to worry about then. With the blackness around you and the sound of your mate's breathing on your right and the same for the man on your left—the slow move forward, trying to feel out what dirty tricks the Greenie techs had thought of this time to guard their sleep . . . the quick strike—and the pounding drive back to the boat with nothing to guide you through the dark but the supersonics in your head bones—

He wanted to go back.

He went to see Phipps about it, sought him out in his office. "You, eh? Have a cigarette."

"No, thanks."

"Real tobacco—none of your 'crazy weed.'"

"No, thanks, I don't use 'em."

"Well, maybe you've got something. The way my mouth tastes these mornings—" Phipps lit up himself, sat back and waited.

Don said, "Look—you're the boss around here."

Phipps exhaled, then said carefully, "Let's say I'm the co-ordinator. I certainly don't try to boss the technical work."

Don brushed it aside. "You're the boss for my purposes.

See here, Mr. Phipps, I feel useless around here. Can you arrange to get me back to my outfit?"

Phipps carefully made a smoke ring. "I'm sorry you feel that way. I could give you work to do. You could be an executive assistant to me."

Don shook his head. "I've had enough of 'pick up sticks and lay them straight.' I want real work—my own work. I'm a soldier and there's a war going on—that's where I belong. Now when can I get transportation?"

"You can't."

"Huh?"

"Mr. Harvey, I can't let you go; you know too much. If you had turned over the ring without asking questions, you could have gone back to your outfit the next hour—but you had to know, you had to know everything. Now we don't dare risk your capture. You know the Greenies put every prisoner through full interrogation; we can't dare risk that—not yet."

"But—Dog take it, sir, I'll never be captured! I made up my mind about that a long time ago."

Phipps shrugged. "If you get yourself killed, that's all right. But we can't be sure of that, no matter how resolute you are. We can't risk it; there's too much at stake."

"You can't hold me here! You have no authority over me!"

"No. But you can't leave."

Don opened his mouth, closed it, and walked out.

He woke up the next morning determined to do something about it. But Dr. Conrad was up before he was and stopped to make a suggestion before he left. "Don?"

"Yeah, Rog?"

"If you can tear yourself out of that sack, you might come around to the power lab this morning. There will be something worth looking at—I think."

"Huh? What? What time?"

"Oh, say about nine o'clock."

Don showed up, along with apparently every human in the place and about half of Sir Isaac's numerous family. Roger Conrad was in charge of the demonstration. He was busy at a control console which told the uninstructed observer nothing. He busied himself with adjustments, looked up and said, "Just keep your eyes on the birdie, folks—right over that bench." He pressed a key.

There flicked into being over the bench, hanging in the air unsupported, a silvery ball some two feet across. It seemed to be a perfect sphere and a perfect reflector and, more than anything else in the world, it made Don think of a Christmas tree ornament. Conrad grinned triumphantly. "Okay, Tony—give it the ax!"

Tony Vincente, the most muscular of the laboratory crew, picked up a broad-bladed ax he had ready. "How would you like it split—up and down, or sideways?"

"Suit yourself."

Vincente swung the ax over his head and brought it down hard.

It bounced off.

The sphere did not quiver, nor was there any mar on its perfect mirror surface. Conrad's boyish grin got even wider. "End of act one," he announced and pressed another button. The sphere disappeared, left nothing to show where it had been.

Conrad bent over his controls. "Act two," he announced. "We now cancel out half the locus. Stand clear of the bench." Shortly he looked up. "Ready! Aim! Fire!" Another shape took being, a perfect sphere otherwise like the last. Its curved outer surface was faced up. "Stick the props in, Tony."

"Just a sec, while I light up." Vincente lit a cigarette, puffed it vigorously, then propped it in an ash tray and slid it under the half globe. Conrad again manipulated his controls; the shape descended, rested on the bench, covering the burning cigarette on its tray. "Anybody want to try the ax on it, or anything else?" asked Conrad.

Nobody seemed anxious to tamper with the unknown. Conrad again operated his board and the silver bowl lifted. The cigarette still smoldered in the tray, unaffected. "How," he asked, "would you like to put a lid like that over the Federation's capital at Bermuda—and leave it in place until they decided to come to terms?"

175

The idea quite evidently met with unanimous approval. The members of the Organization present were all, or almost all, citizens of Venus, emotionally involved in the rebellion no matter what else they were doing. Phipps cut through the excited comment with a question. "Dr. Conrad!—would you give us a popular explanation of what we have seen? Why it works, I mean; we can guess at its enormous potentials."

Conrad's face got very serious. "Mmm . . . Chief, perhaps it would be clearest to say that the fasarta modulates the garbab in such a phase relationship that the thrimaleen is forced to bast—or, to put it another way, somebody loosed mice in the washroom. Seriously, there is no popular way to explain it. If you were willing to spend five hard years with me, working up through the math, I could probably bring you to the same level of ignorance and confusion that I enjoy. Some of the tensor equations involved are, to put it mildly, unique. But the instructions were clear enough and we did it."

Phipps nodded. "Thanks—if that is the word I want. I'll ask Sir Isaac."

"Do, please. I'd like to listen."

Despite the proof that the lab crew had been able to jury-rig at least part of the equipment described by the message in the two wires, Don's jitters got no better. Each day the sign in the mess hall reminded him that time was running out—and that he was sucking his thumb while it did so. He thought no more about trying to get them to send him back to the war zone; instead he began to make plans to get there on his own.

He had seen maps of the Great South Sea and knew roughly where he was. To the north there was territory uninhabited even by dragons—but not uninhabited by their carnivorous cousins. It was considered impassable. The way to the south around the lower end of the sea was much farther, but it was dragon country all the way right up to outlying human farms. With whistle speech and food enough to last at least a week he might get through to some settler who could pass him along to the next. As for the rest he had his knife and he had his wits and he was much more swampwise than he had been when he had made his escape from Bankfield's men.

He began to sneak food out of the mess hall and cache it in his room.

He was within a day and a night of attempting his break when Phipps sent for him. He considered not showing up but decided that it would be less suspicion-arousing to comply.

"Sit down," Phipps began. "Cigarette? No—I forgot. What have you been doing with yourself lately? Keeping busy?"

"Not a darn thing to do!"

"Sorry. Mr. Harvey, have you given any thought to what sort of a world we will have when this is over?"

"Well, no, not exactly." He had thought about it, but his own imaginings were too poorly worked out for him to care to express them. As for himself, someday the war would be over—he supposed—and then he would carry out his long-postponed intention of seeking out his parents. After that, well——

"What sort of world would you like it to be?"

"Uh? Well, I don't know." Don pondered. "I guess I'm not what you call 'politically minded.' I don't much care how they run it—except, well, there ought to be a sort of *looseness* about it. You know—a man ought to be able to do what he wants to, if he can, and not be pushed around."

Phipps nodded. "You and I have more in common than you may have thought. I'm not a purist in political theory myself. Any government that gets to be too big and too successful gets to be a nuisance. The Federation got that way—it started out decently enough—and now it has to be trimmed down to size. So that the citizens can enjoy some 'looseness.'"

Don said, "Maybe the dragons have the right idea—no organization bigger than a family."

Phipps shook his head. "What's right for dragons is not right for us. Anyhow, families can be just as oppressive as government—take a look at the youngsters around here; five hundred years or so to look forward to before they can sneeze without permission. I asked your opinion because I don't know the answer myself—and I've studied the dynamics of history longer than you've been alive. All I know is that we are about to turn loose into the world forces the outcome of which I cannot guess."

Don looked startled. "We've got space travel now; I don't see what important difference it will make to make it faster. As for the other gimmick, it seems to me a swell idea to be able to put a lid on a city so that it can't be atombombed."

"Granted. But that is just the beginning. I've been making a list of some of the things that will come about—I think. In the first place you vastly underestimate the importance of speeding up transportation. As for the other possibilities, I'm stumped. I'm too old and my imagination needs greasing. But here's one for a starter: we might be able to move water, lots of water, significant amounts, from here to Mars." His brow wrinkled. "We might even be able to move planets themselves."

Don looked up suddenly. Somewhere he had heard almost those same words . . . the memory evaded him.

"But never mind," Phipps went on. "I was just trying to get a younger, fresher viewpoint. You might think about it. Those laboratory laddies won't, that's sure. These physicists—they produce wonders but they never know what other wonders their wonders will beget." He paused and added, "We are resetting the clock, but we don't know what time it will be."

When he added nothing more Don decided with relief that the interview was over and started to get up. "No, no, don't go," Phipps put in. "I had another matter on my mind. You've been getting ready to leave, haven't you?"

Don stuttered and stammered. "What gave you that idea?"

"I'm right. Some morning we would wake up and find your bed empty. Then I'd be put to a lot of trouble when effort can't be spared to try to find you and bring you back."

Don relaxed. "Conrad snitched to you," he said bitterly.

"Conrad? No. I doubt if the good doctor ever notices anything larger than an electron. No, credit me with some sense. My business is people. True, I did badly with you when you first arrived—but I still plead that I was bone weary. Tiredness is a mild insanity. The point is: you're leaving and I can't stop you. I know dragons well enough to know that Sir Isaac wouldn't let me if you wanted to go. You're 'his' confounded 'egg'! But I can't let you go; the reasons are just as compelling as before. So—rather than let you go, I'd have to try to kill you."

Don leaned forward, shifting his weight onto his feet. "Do you think you could?" he said very softly.

Phipps grinned. "No, I don't. That's why I've had to think up another scheme. You know that we are making up the ship's crew. How would you like to go along?"

XVIII

Little David

Don let his mouth drop open and left it that way. To his credit, while he had thought about it, he had never given it the slightest serious consideration; he was not conceited enough to think that he would be allowed to hitch a ride, just to suit his personal wishes, on *this* trip.

Phipps went on, "Frankly, I'm doing it to get rid of you, to put you on ice, safe from the Federation's inquisitors, until it no longer matters. But I think I can justify it. We want to train as many as the *Little David* can carry on this trip as cadres for more ships. But my choice is limited—most of our group here are too old, or they are near-sighted, narrow-chested young geniuses suitable only for laboratories. You are young, you are healthy, your reflexes are fast—I know! —and you are space-wise from babyhood. True, you are not a qualified shiphandler, but that won't matter too much; these ships will be new to everyone. Mr. Harvey, how would you like to go to Mars—and return as 'Captain Harvey,' master of your own ship—a ship strong enough to strike at these Federation vermin orbiting around Venus?

"Or executive officer, at least," Phipps qualified, reflecting that in a two-man ship Don could hardly be less.

Like it? He'd love it! Don's tongue got twisted trying to

accept too quickly. Then almost at once he was struck by a cold thought; Phipps saw from his expression that something was wrong. "What's the matter?" Phipps said sharply. "Are you afraid?"

"Afraid?" Don looked annoyed. "Of course I'll be afraid—I've been afraid so many times that I am no longer scared to be afraid again. That's not the trouble."

"What is it, then? Speak up!"

"It's just this—I'm still on active duty. I can't go gallivanting off a hundred million miles or so. Properly speaking, it would be desertion. Why, when they laid hands on me, they'd probably hang me first and ask questions afterwards."

Phipps relaxed. "Oh. Perhaps that can be managed. You let me worry about it."

It could be managed. It was only three days later that Don received new orders, written this time, and delivered by devious means that he could only guess at. They read:

To: Harvey, Donald J., Sergeant-Specialist 1/c
Via: Channels

1. You are assigned to special temporary duty of indefinite duration.

2. You will travel as necessary to carry out this duty.

3. This assignment is deemed in the best interests of the Republic. When, in your opinion, your duties are completed, you will report to the nearest competent authority and request transportation to enable you to report in person to the Chief of Staff.

4. For the duration of this duty you are brevetted to the rank of sublieutenant.

J. S. Busby, Wing Colonel (brevet)
For the Commanding General

First Endorsement:
1. Delivered (via courier)

Henry Marsten, Captain (brevet)
Commanding 16th Gondola Combat Team

Clipped to the orders was a scrawled note which read:

P.S.   Dear "Lieutenant,"
These are the silliest orders I have ever had to endorse.
What the devil have you been up to? Did you marry one
of the dragons? Or did you catch a Big Brass with his finger off his number? Anyway, have fun—and good hunting!
                                                        Marsten

Don tucked the orders and the note into his pocket.
Every now and then he would reach in and touch them.

The days trickled away; the dotted line got ever closer
to Mars: and the whole group got more and more jumpy.
Another date was posted on the mess hall wall, a date by
which the *Little David* must be ready—if they were to arrive
in time.

The calendar marked that deadline the day the ship
was finally manned. At raise-ship-minus-twenty-minutes Don
was still in Sir Isaac's study, his baggage (such as it was)
already aboard. Saying goodbye to Sir Isaac, he discovered,
was rather more difficult than he had expected it to be.
His head was not cluttered with ideas about "father im-
ages" and the like; he was simply aware that this dragon
was all the family he had, much more so than that remote
pair on the planet where he was headed.

He was almost relieved when a glance at his watch
told him that he was late. "Got to run," he said. "Nine-
teen minutes."

"Yes, my dear Donald. Your short-lived race must always
live in frantic haste."

"Well—g'bye."

"Farewell, Mist on the Waters."

He stopped outside Sir Isaac's study to blow his nose
and pull himself together. Isobel stepped out from behind
a massive pillar. "Don—I wanted to say goodbye to you."

"Huh? Sure, sure—but aren't you coming out to see 'raise
ship'?"

"No."

"Well, as you like, but I've got to hurry, Grandma."

"I told you to stop calling me 'Grandma'!"

"So you fibbed about your age. So you're stuck with it—Grandma."

"Don, you stubborn beast! Don—you come back. You understand me?"

"Why, sure! We'll be back in jig time."

"See that you do! You're not bright enough to take care of yourself. Well— Open sky!" She grabbed him by both ears and kissed him quickly, then ran away.

Don stared after her, rubbing his mouth. Girls, he reflected, were much odder than dragons. Probably another race entirely. He hurried on down to the take-off point. The entire colony seemed to be there and he was the last of the crew to arrive, winning thereby a dirty look from Captain Rhodes, skipper of the *Little David*. Rhodes, once of Interplanet and now of the Middle Guard, had appeared three days ago; he had not been inclined to talk and had spent the whole time with Conrad. Don touched the pocket and wondered if Rhodes carried orders that read as oddly as his.

The *Little David* had been dragged up on shore, where she rested in skids. No catapult would be needed for her take-off nor was any available; the three shuttle catapults on Venus were all in the hands of the Federation forces. The ship had been concealed by a screen of boughs; these were now cut back, giving her open sky, room to lift.

Don looked at her, thinking that she looked more like an over-sized and unusually ugly concrete mixer than a space ship. The roots of her amputated wings stubbed out sadly to port and starboard. Her needle nose had been trimmed off and replaced by a bulbous special radar housing. She was scarred here and there by the marks of cutting torches where modifications had been done hastily and with no attempt to pretty up, smooth out, and make ship-shape after the surgery.

Her rocket tubes were gone and the space formerly occupied by rocket fuel tanks now held an atomic power pile, while a major part of what had been her passenger space was now taken up by a massive bulkhead, the anti-radiation shield to protect the crew from the deadly emanations of the pile. All over her outer surface, disfiguring what had been sleek streamlines, were bulging discoids—"antennas" Conrad had called them, antennas used to strain the very shape of space. They did not look much like antennas to Don.

The *Little David* carried a crew of nine, Rhodes, Conrad, Harvey, and six others, all young and all on "makee-learnee"—except Roger Conrad who carried the undignified title of "Gadget Officer," that being shorter than "Officer in Charge of Special Appliances." She carried one passenger, Old Malath. He was not in sight and Don did not look for him; the after part of the remaining cabin space had been sealed off for his use and air-conditioned thin, dry, and cold.

All were aboard, the lock was sealed, and Don sat down. Despite the space taken up by the new equipment enough passenger seats had been left in the little ship to accommodate them. Captain Rhodes settled himself in his control seat and barked, "Acceleration stations! Fasten belts!" Don did so.

Rhodes turned to Conrad who was still standing. Conrad said conversationally, "About two minutes, gentlemen. Since we had no time for a test run, this will be a very interesting experiment. Any of three things can happen." He paused.

Rhodes snapped, "Yes? Go on!"

"First, nothing might happen. We might bog down on a slight theoretical oversight. Second, it might work. And third—it might blow up." He grinned. "Anyone want to place a small bet?"

Nobody answered. He glanced down and said, "Okay, Captain—twist her tail!"

It seemed to Don that it had suddenly become night and that they had gone immediately into free fall. His stomach, long used to the fairly high gravity of Venus, lurched and complained. Conrad, not strapped down, was floating, anchored by one hand to his control board. "Sorry, gentlemen!" he said. "Slight oversight. Now let's adjust this locus to Mars normal, as an accommodation to our passenger." He fiddled with his dials.

Don's stomach went abruptly back into place as a quite satisfactory weight of more than one-third g took over. Conrad said, "Very well, Captain, you can let them unstrap."

Someone behind Don said, "What's the matter? Didn't it work?"

Conrad said, "Oh, yes, it worked. In fact we have been accelerating at about—" He stopped to study his dials. "—twenty gravities ever since we left the atmosphere."

The ship remained surrounded by darkness, cut off from the rest of the universe by what was inadequately described as a "discontinuity," save for a few minutes every other watch when Conrad cut the field to enable Captain Rhodes to see out and thereby take direct star sights. During these periods they were in free fall and the stars shone sharp through the ports. Then the darkness again would close in and the *Little David* would revert to a little world of its own.

Captain Rhodes showed a persisting tendency to swear softly to himself after each fix and to work his calculations through at least three times.

In between times Conrad conducted "gadget class" for as many hours each day as he could stand it. Don found most of the explanations as baffling as the one Conrad had given Phipps. "I just don't get it, Rog," he confessed after their instructor had been over the same point three times.

Conrad shrugged and grinned. "Don't let it throw you. By the time you have helped install the equipment in your own ship, you'll know it the way your foot knows your shoe. Meantime, let's run through it again."

Aside from instructions there was nothing to do and the ship was too small and too crowded in any case. A card game ran almost continuously. Don had very little money to start with; very soon he had none and was no longer part of the game. He slept and he thought.

Phipps had been right, he decided; travel at this speed would change things—people would go planet-jumping as casually as they now went from continent to continent on Earth. It would be like—well, like the change from sailing ships to trans-ocean rockets, only the change would be over-night, instead of spread over three centuries.

Maybe he would go back to Earth someday; Earth had its points—horseback riding, for instance. He wondered if Lazy still remembered him?

He'd like to teach Isobel to ride a horse. He'd like to see her face when she first laid eyes on a horse!

One thing he knew: he would not stay on Earth, even if he did go back. Nor would he stay on Venus—nor on Mars. He knew now where he belonged—in space, where he was born. Any planet was merely a hotel to him; space was his home.

Maybe he would go out in the *Pathfinder*, out to the stars. He had a sneaking hunch that, if they came through this stunt alive, a member of the original crew of the *Little David* would be able to wangle it to be chosen for the Long Trip. Of course, the *Pathfinder* was limited to married couples only, but that was not an obstacle. He was certain that he would be married in time to qualify although he could not remember clearly just when he had come by that knowledge. And Isobel was the whither-thou-goest sort; she wouldn't hold him back. The *Pathfinder* would not leave right away in any case; they would wait to change over to the Horst-Milne-Conrad drive, once they knew about it.

In any event he meant to stir around a bit, do some traveling, once the war was over. They would surely have to transfer him to the High Guard when he got back, then High Guard experience would stand him in good stead when he was a discharged veteran. Come to think about it, maybe he was already in the High Guard, so to speak.

McMasters had certainly been right; there was just one way to get to Mars—in a spacing task force.

He looked around him. The inevitable card game was still in progress and two of his mates were shooting dice on the deckplates, the cubes spinning lazily in the low para-gravity field. Conrad had opened up his chair and was stretched out asleep, his mouth open. He decided that it certainly did not look like a world-saving task force; the place had more the air of an unmade bed.

They were due to "come out" on the eleventh day, within easy free fall of Mars, and—if all guesses had been right—close by the Federation task force, making almost a photo finish with those ships. "Gadget class" gave way to drill at battle stations. Rhodes picked Art Frankel, who had had some shiphandling experience, as his co-pilot; Conrad was assisted by Franklyn Chiang, a physicist like himself. Of the other four, two were on radio, two on radar. Don's battle station was a saddle amidships, back of the pilots' chairs—the "dead man's" seat. Here he guarded a spring-loaded demolition switch, a type of switch known through the centuries as a "dead-man" switch for the contrary reason that it operated only if its operator were dead.

At first drill Conrad got the others squared away, then came back to Don's station. "You savvy what you are to do, Don?"

"Sure. I throw this switch to arm the bomb, then I hang onto the dead-man switch."

"No, no! Grab the dead-man switch *first*—then close the arming switch."

"Yes, sure. I just said it backwards."

"Be sure you don't do it backwards! Just remember this, Lieutenant: if you let go, *everything* does."

"Okay. Say, Rog, this thing triggers an A-bomb—right?"

"Wrong. We should waste so much money! But the load of H.E. in there is plenty for a little can like this, I assure you. So, anxious as we are to blow up this packet rather than let it be captured, *don't* let go of that switch otherwise. If you feel a need to scratch, rise above it."

Captain Rhodes came aft and with a motion of his head sent Conrad forward. He spoke to Don in a low voice, such that his words did not reach the others. "Harvey, are you satisfied with this assignment? You don't mind it?"

"No, I don't mind," Don answered. "I know the others all have more technical training than I have. This is my speed."

"That's not what I mean," the Captain corrected. "You could fill any of the other seats, except mine and Dr. Conrad's. I want to be sure you can do this job."

"I don't see why not. Grab onto this switch, and then

186

close that one—and hang on for dear life. It sure doesn't take any higher mathematics to do that."

"That's still not what I mean. I don't know you, Harvey. I understand you have had combat experience. These others haven't—which is why you have this job. Those who do know you think you can do it. I'm not worried that you might forget to hang on; what I want to know is this: if it becomes necessary to *let go* of that switch, can you do it?"

Don answered almost at once—but not before there had been time for him to think of several things—Dr. Jefferson, who had almost certainly suicided, not simply died—Old Charlie with his mouth quivering but his cleaver hand steady and sure—and an undying voice ringing through the fog, "*Venus and Freedom!*"

"Guess I can if I have to."

"Good. I'm by no means sure that I could. I'm depending on you, sir, if worse comes to worst, not to let my ship be captured." He went forward.

Tension mounted, tempers got edgy. They had no way to be sure that they would come out near the Federation task force; that force might be using something other than what was assumed to be the maximum-performance orbit. They could not even be certain that the Federation forces were not already on Mars, already in command and difficult to dislodge. The *Little David's* laboratory miracles were designed for ship-to-ship encounter in space, not for mopping up on the surface of a planet.

Conrad had another worry, one that he did not voice, that the ship's weapons might not work as planned. More than any of the rest he knew the weakness of depending on theoretical predictions. He knew how frequently the most brilliant computations were confounded by previously unsuspected natural laws. There was no substitute for test—and these weapons had not been tested. He lost his habitual grin and even got into a bad-tempered difference of opinion with Rhodes as to the calculated time of "coming out."

The difference of opinion was finally settled; a half hour later Rhodes said quietly, "It's almost time, gentlemen. Battle stations." He went to his own seat, strapped himself in, and snapped, "Report!"

"Co-pilot."

"Radio!"

"Radar!"

"Special weapons ready."

"Dead man!" Don finished.

There was a long wait while the seconds oozed slowly away. Rhodes spoke quietly into a microphone, warning Malath to be ready for free fall, then called out, "Stand by!" Don took a tighter grip on the demolition switch.

Suddenly he was weightless; ahead of him and in the passenger ports on each side the stars burst into being. He could not see Mars and decided that it must be "under" the ship. The Sun was somewhere aft; it was not in his eyes. But his view ahead was excellent; the *Little David*, having begun life as a winged shuttle, had an airplane-type conning port in front of the piloting chairs. Don's position let him see as clearly as Rhodes and his co-pilot and much better than could the others.

"Radar?" inquired Rhodes.

"Take it easy, Skipper. Even the speed of light is— Oh, oh! *Blips!*"

"Co-ordinates and range!"

"Theta three five seven point two; phi minus zero point eight; range radius six eight oh——"

"I'm feeding it in automatically," Conrad cut in sharply.

"Tracking?"

"Not yet."

"In range?"

"No. I think we should sit tight and close range as much as possible. They may not have seen us."

They had slowed their headlong flight earlier to permit maneuvering; nevertheless they were closing with the "blips" at more than ninety miles a second. Don strained his eyes to try to make out the ships, if such the radar reflections were. No use—his protoplasmic scanners were no match for electronic ones.

They stayed that way, nerves on edge and stomachs tight, and range steadily closing, until it seemed that the blips must not be the task force, perhaps were even some wandering uncharted asteroid—when the radio alarm, sweeping automatically the communication frequencies, clangingly broke the silence. "Get it!" shouted Rhodes.

"Coming up." There was a short wait. "They demanded that we identify. They're our babies, all right."

"Switch it over here." Rhodes turned to Conrad. "How about it?"

"I ought to be closer. Stall 'em!" Conrad's face was grey and wet with sweat.

Rhodes touched a key and spoke into his mike. "What ship are *you*? Identify yourself."

The answer was amplified through the horn over the Captain's head. "Identify or be fired upon."

Rhodes glanced again at Conrad, who was too busy to look back. Rhodes spoke into the mike, "This is the destroyer *Little David*, commissioned privateer, Venus Republic. Surrender immediately."

Don strained his eyes again. It seemed to him that there were three new "stars" dead ahead.

The answer came back with hardly more than transmission delay. "Federation flagship *Peacemaker* to pirate ship *Little David*: surrender or be destroyed."

To Rhodes' inquiry Conrad turned a face contorted with uncertainty. "It's still pretty far. The track hunts on me. I might miss."

"No time! Go ahead!"

Don could see them now—ships, growing unbelievably. Then, most suddenly, one was a silver globe, then a second—and a third. A cluster of incredible, Gargantuan Christmas tree ornaments where had been three mighty warships, they continued to swell, drew to the left and flashed past the ship . . . the "battle" was over.

Conrad sighed shakily. "That's all, Captain." He turned and said, "Don, you'd make us all feel easier if you'd open that arming switch. We're not going to need it."

Mars swam below them, ruddy and beautiful. Schiaparelli Station, I. T. & T.'s powerful interplanetary radio, had already had a silvery "hat" placed on it to guard the secret of their strike; Captain Rhodes had spoken with a lesser station, warning of their arrival. In less than an hour they would ground near da Thon—Malath himself had come out of his icebox, no longer sick and weary but pert as a cricket, willing to risk the warm, thick, moist air of the cabin for a view of home.

Don climbed back into his battle-station saddle for a better view. The fabulous *canali* were already plain to the eye; he could see them cutting through the soft greens and the dominant orange and brick red. It was winter in the south; the planet wore its south pole cap jauntily, like a chef's hat. The fancy reminded him of Old Charlie; he thought of him with gentle melancholy, memory softened by all that had gone between.

Mars at last . . . he'd be seeing his parents perhaps before the day was out—and give his father the ring. This was certainly not the way they had planned it.

Next time he would try not to take the long way round.

ROBERT A.
HEINLEIN

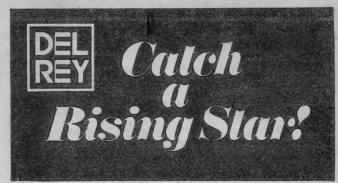

DEL REY *Catch a Rising Star!*

Jack L. Chalker

A JUNGLE OF STARS	25457	1.50
THE WEB OF THE CHOZEN	27376	1.75
MIDNIGHT AT THE WELL OF SOULS	25768	1.95
DANCERS IN THE AFTERGLOW	27564	1.75

James P. Hogan

INHERIT THE STARS	25704	1.50
THE GENESIS MACHINE	27231	1.75
THE GENTLE GIANTS OF GANYMEDE	27375	1.75

Tony Rothman

THE WORLD IS ROUND	27213	1.95